ALL WE HAVE

Haven's Bay Holiday Series

J.H. CROIX

"My heart is and always will be yours." -Jane Austen, Pride and Prejudice

Sign up for my newsletter for information on new releases & get a FREE copy of one of my books!

http://jhcroixauthor.com/subscribe/

Follow me!
jhcroix@jhcroix.com
https://amazon.com/author/jhcroix
https://www.bookbub.com/authors/j-h-croix
https://www.facebook.com/jhcroix
https://www.instagram.com/jhcroix/

Reader's Note: a short version of this story (16,000-ish words) was released as part of a time-limited free anthology, All I Want Is You, in Nov 2021. That anthology was only available for a limited time through Bookfunnel and was not available on any retailer. This expanded version is over 44,000 words.

Chapter One

JANE

My headlights glowed through the blowing snow, offering a short path of light to guide me and nothing more. I had to keep reminding myself that was all I needed.

I wasn't even sure where the edge of the road was anymore. The weather was definitely *not* cooperating with my plans for a relaxing vacation in my hometown of Haven's Bay, Maine. I just had to get to the end of this driveway. Of course, I also needed this to be the correct driveway. Small favors and all that.

I loosened one hand on the steering wheel, stretching my fingers before curling them back around and repeating the motion with my other hand. It had been snowing steadily for the last hour and a half of my drive here from Boston.

"Yes," I whispered to myself when I looked ahead and saw what I thought was the right house situated at the end of the driveway. I couldn't see beyond its hulking shadow through the snow, and I couldn't see the ocean that I knew lay just beyond it. Hell, I couldn't see much of anything.

I carefully steered my car around the circle at the end of the driveway, slowing where my lights angled toward the entrance. I came to a quiet stop, the snow cushioning the sound of my tires. Putting my car in park, I took several deep breaths. Normally, I would turn my car off. But right now, the only light available came from my headlights. I zipped my down jacket and stuffed my knit hat on top of my head before fishing the house key out of my purse.

Curling my hand around the single key, I left my car lights on and climbed out, my boots promptly sinking into the fluffy snow on the drive. I navigated the front steps carefully. I let out a breath I hadn't realized I'd been holding when the key slid into the lock on the massive front door smoothly.

The sound of the doorway opening echoed in the hallway. I tapped my boots on the threshold, knocking the snow loose as I stepped inside. I shivered as I glanced around, trying to get my bearings. Reaching to the side, I felt for a light switch. When I didn't find it on one side, I moved to the other, relieved when my hand found the familiar shape. My relief expanded when the lights actually came on. I closed the door behind me, my gaze arcing around the entryway.

"Wow," I breathed.

I took a quick walk down memory lane, elicited by nothing more than stepping inside this old house. The entryway was two stories high with a staircase curving along the wall that led to the upper floor. Back in high school, I spent afternoons here with my friends, Thea, Audrey, and Sasha. The space felt echoey now. Thea had warned me that most of the furniture had been sold off at one point and that she and her brothers were gradually refurnishing the place.

After spinning in a slow circle, I began walking

down the hallway after flicking on another light. My footsteps echoed on the hardwood floors. I discovered a comfy-looking sofa in the living room. I smiled when I saw chopped wood neatly stacked in a decorative rack beside the fireplace. That would warm me up.

Sliding my phone out of my pocket, I pulled up the text exchange I'd recently had with Thea.

Me: *I made it. The key worked, and the lights are on. Thank you so much.*

I hit send and slipped my phone back into my pocket. I did a quick loop around the downstairs, making sure to turn the thermostats up. I peered out the back window into the yard that stretched to the ocean. For now, all I could see was blowing snow.

I hurried back out to my car to fetch my purse and bag and turn the car off. After I got back inside, I realized a small flaw in my plan. I didn't have any food with me, and I was starving. After I searched out the bedroom situation upstairs, I took the room closest to the bathroom. Leaving my bag there, I made my way back into the kitchen to see if maybe there was some food in the cabinets.

Thea had told me she and her brothers came up several times a year, so I thought something might be here. I smiled when I found some dry goods in the otherwise lightly stocked pantry. I could always make some chicken soup straight from the can. My phone vibrated in my pocket, and I slipped it out to see a reply from Thea.

Thea: *Awesome. Glad you made it. Hope you get that peace and quiet you're looking for. Good luck dealing with your parents' house. Text or call if you need anything.*

I sent a thumbs-up and a heart back.

Me: *Thanks again.*

Setting my phone on the counter, I stilled when I

heard the front door opening, the sound echoing down the hallway. What the hell?

A subtle frisson of fear chased up my spine. I didn't want this to turn into a horror movie where the single woman on vacation faces a litany of creepy things.

"Hello?" a man's voice called.

My heart was pounding unsteadily, but I had no choice but to investigate. I turned and walked toward the hallway. Just as I reached the archway that led into the kitchen, the man in question appeared.

My pulse stuttered and then lunged as I stared up at Ian Tate. Ian was one of Thea's brothers. He'd been a few years ahead of us in high school. My eyes chased over him. Time had been generous to Ian, considering that nature had already been ridiculously generous. His black hair was mussed and damp from the snow. His piercing green eyes stared at me, his gaze calculating. He seemed taller than I recalled, but I hadn't seen him in at least ten years. His broad shoulders filled out his winter jacket. It was unzipped, and I couldn't help but notice that his navy-blue T-shirt outlined his muscled chest. He was wearing faded black jeans and gave off an intimidating air.

He looked annoyed. "Who the hell are you?" he asked.

Of course, Ian wouldn't remember me. Even though I'd been one of his sister's friends growing up, I doubted he paid much attention to me. God, he'd been so annoying in high school—handsome and popular with girls flocking to him.

Meanwhile, I'd been the nerdy, quiet girl, a little too shy to shine socially in the cutthroat world of high school. I'd had a tight circle of friends but didn't venture beyond that. If he'd ever noticed me beyond occasionally seeing me here when I was with Thea, I doubted it would register in his memory. He'd been too popular for a girl like me.

I was different now, though. I wasn't shy, and I didn't care to impress guys like him anymore. I rested a hand on my hip and arched a brow. "You don't remember me, Ian?"

I willed my pulse to pump the brakes and slow the hell down because my hormones did *not* need to be getting all excited over Ian Tate.

Chapter Two

IAN

The woman standing in front of me gave me an imperious look with her hand resting on her hip and her chin lifted. She arched one brow, her lips twisting to the side. I definitely didn't remember her at a glance. Although, a memory pinged. I tried to grasp it, but I couldn't quite place her.

"Maybe I do," I said smoothly, not willing to admit she might be right.

"What's my name then?" she prompted, her gaze cool as her eyes swept up and down.

Although she was giving off a good impression of not being rattled, I didn't miss the flush high on her cheekbones and the rapid beat of her pulse, visible at the base of her throat. Her honey-blond hair was twisted into a knot on top of her head with loose tendrils framing her face. She wore a pair of bright blue glasses. Her eyes were a unique hazel, almost iridescent, the blue and green changing with the light.

I was tired, too fucking tired, to try to play it cool. I shrugged. "I'm sorry I don't know your name. You, apparently, know mine, so I'm assuming you also know this home belongs to my family."

She blinked at me behind those glasses, her hand dropping from her hip. "Yes, I know this is your family's home. Thea told me I could stay here for three weeks. She gave me a key. Since you don't seem to remember, I'm Jane, Jane Matthews. Thea and I were friends growing up."

The minute she said her name, the memory clicked into place. Jane was Thea's pretty friend who almost always had her nose buried in a book. She wasn't a huge fan of eye contact back then. She didn't seem to have a problem with it now as she steadily held my gaze.

"Did she now?" I returned. "Well, she forgot to mention that to me. I'll be here through January."

Jane blinked again, her nose wrinkling as she considered my reply. "Well, it looks like I'll have to find somewhere else to stay then. Thea obviously didn't know you would be here."

I shook my head. "No, she didn't. Shocking as it may sound, I don't keep my little sister apprised of everything I do."

She rolled her eyes as she turned, crossing the kitchen to close the pantry. "I was just about to make some chicken soup because I'm starving. I'll have to call around and see where else I can stay."

I was replying before I thought better of it. "It's terrible out. You can't do that. Plus, this is Haven's Bay in the middle of winter. It's not like there are tons of places to stay. Most places are closed."

Jane spun around to face me. "Tell me something I don't know," she snapped.

"Look, you're Thea's friend, and this is a big house.

We'll figure it out. I'm not gonna let you drive out in that snow. Trust me, it's only getting worse."

"Really?" she asked as she crossed over to the windows to peer out into the snowy darkness.

She turned on the light outside on the corner of the house, her eyes widening. The light illuminated nothing but blowing snow. It was wet, thick, and heavy now. I called this kind of snow "snot" snow. It made the roads slick, and tires tended to smear over the surface of it. I'd driven on winter roads for most of my life. Short of black ice, this was the worst kind of snow for driving. Add in the poor visibility and questionable traction along with the wind and it created dangerous conditions. There was no way I would let Jane go out in this weather at this hour.

She turned back toward me, pursing her lips as she contemplated. "It's probably not a good idea for me to go out."

"It's *definitely* not a good idea for you to go out. I'm starving too," I added. "I'll get my bags. Which bedroom did you take?"

She glanced back at me. "The one toward the front. Is that okay?"

"Of course, it's okay. There are five bedrooms up there."

"Are you sure?"

"I'm sure, Jane."

I didn't wait for her reply and walked back down the hallway, my footsteps echoing through the downstairs. A few minutes later, I dropped my bags in the master bedroom, changed into something more comfortable, and made my way back downstairs. When I walked into the kitchen, Jane had a drawer open and was perusing the pots and pans.

"Is chicken soup all we have?" I asked as I crossed over to peer into the pantry myself.

"That's the only quick option."

"I'm going to check the freezer in the basement. Maybe we have something there."

"Is that okay?" she asked.

I paused in the doorway. "I don't see why not."

Jane's cheeks went pink, sending a sizzle down my spine as I looked at her. Wow, that was interesting. "I'll be right back."

Ignoring my body's reaction to her, I jogged down into the basement, flicking on the lights and crossing over to the new chest freezer I'd purchased last summer when I was here with my two brothers and my sister. I was pleased to find a few options, including a pan of pre-made lasagna. Maybe it wasn't homemade, but I was fucking starving, and it was freezing outside—perfect weather for lasagna. There was even a loaf of frozen French bread and some butter.

I jogged back upstairs with the items in hand, calling, "We've got frozen lasagna and bread. Let's have an actual meal."

Jane's eyes widened as she looked over. "Are you serious?"

"Sure am. Crank that oven on."

Jane crossed over and turned on the oven. In short order, we had wrapped the frozen bread in foil, and Jane put it in the oven, explaining it would thaw while the oven heated. I discovered her to be efficient and found we worked easily together. After the lasagna was in the oven, Jane melted butter and seasoned it with parsley and a dash of garlic powder to pour on the bread.

I peered into the cabinet where we kept the wine,

smiling when I discovered several bottles of good red wine waiting for us. "Would you like some wine?"

"There's wine too?" she asked, a hint of surprise in her tone.

"Absolutely," I said as I chose a bottle. "Will this work for you?" I held up a bottle of Merlot from a local winery.

Her eyes widened as a slow smile stretched across her face, sending electricity through me in a fiery shimmer. Jesus. I knew I'd been overworked and over-stressed, and honestly, so busy that I hadn't even had a casual date in over six months. But still, this reaction was out of place for me.

"Aren't you glad I showed up? You would have made chicken soup and probably not touched anything else here," I teased as I fetched two wine glasses out of the cabinet.

She shrugged as she sat down at the table. "I was planning to go to the store tomorrow, but I also wasn't anticipating all the snow tonight."

I filled our glasses, watching while she took a swallow. She was beautiful. She had tip-tilted eyes behind her glasses and graceful, sleek cheekbones. Her mouth was a little lopsided, and her lips pink and full. She seemed taller than I recalled, now that I remembered her. She and Thea had been a few years behind me in high school, so it made sense she'd be taller now.

After I took my own sip of wine, I asked, "So, how far was your drive?"

"I drove up from Boston, so three and a half hours, or thereabouts. Where did you come from?"

"Washington, DC."

"You drove all the way up today?" Her eyes widened as she rested an elbow on the table and leaned forward.

I shrugged. "I did. Tell me what you do now."

Jane took a sip of wine before replying, "I'm a science professor."

"Oh, what kind of science?"

"Biology and environmental sciences. Even though I drove up from Boston, I just moved there. When I called Thea and told her I had a whole month before I started my new position, she suggested I stay here. I'm getting my parents' house ready to sell. They haven't been there in years, and everything's turned off, so when Thea offered to let me stay here, I took her up on it. What do you do? You're in finance, right?"

"Yup. Investments. In a way, I followed in my father's footsteps, but I'm not all about the fraud."

Jane cast a quick glance at me. "I heard about everything that went down with your dad. I'm really sorry about that."

I took a gulp of wine, shrugging. "It is what it is."

While I wasn't all about the fraud, I'd unintentionally stumbled into it, which was the reason for my vacation or, rather, my need to get away. But I really didn't want to think about that right now, and I certainly wasn't going to get into it with Jane.

"After the storm passes, I'll see what I can figure out about where to stay."

I shook my head quickly. "No need. You're Thea's friend. Even if I didn't expect you here, you don't need to leave, and you don't have many options as it is."

Jane caught a lock of hair that had fallen loose along her neck, spinning it around her forefinger as she eyed me. "Are you sure?"

"I'm positive. It's a big house. Plus, we work well together. We just made lasagna."

Her low chuckle was throaty, and my body tightened instantly in response. Fuck me. I was seriously overworked, and it was addling my hormones. Jane was beautiful, but I wasn't used to reacting to women like this. My dry spell was muddling my brain.

"If cooking frozen lasagna and bread is a major project, I suppose we do work well together," she offered as she waved a hand airily.

I grinned. "You can just ignore me while we're here."

Her brows hitched up. "I can't ignore you. That would be weird and rude. This is *your* family's home," she insisted.

"And you're a guest. Consider it yours while you're here."

"Well, I'll look into my options tomorrow."

"Jane," I warned. "Don't get me in trouble with Thea."

She chuckled again, sending another sizzle through me. "Okay, okay, you're right. She'll give you hell, won't she?"

I nodded. "Have you two stayed in touch all this time?"

"Sporadically. I was living in Seattle for a while. I had a position at a university there, but I was offered a tenure track position in Boston, so I jumped at it. I'll be closer to my parents. It's nice to be back East, and it'll be good to stay in better contact with Thea. She told me Dallas and Noah are also living there. So, you're the only sibling who's not in Boston?" she prompted.

"For now," I replied, thinking that moving there had been on my long-term plan for years now, but I'd only been seriously looking into it recently.

"Are you thinking of moving there?"

"I don't know. I don't have to stay in DC for work,

but I'll figure it out when the timing's right." I left a lot unsaid with that.

DC was filled with politicians, and politicians could be knee-deep in trouble, or so I had learned.

Oblivious to my thoughts, she leaned back in her chair and turned to look out the windows. She took a swallow of wine, and her tongue darted out to swipe across her bottom lip when a drop escaped. My cells tightened again. She was staring out at the blowing snow, which was still illuminated by the light on the corner of the house.

"I haven't been through a nor'easter since we moved away," I offered.

"Me neither."

"Welcome to Haven's Bay," I teased.

She grinned just as the oven buzzer went off. She stood to go check on the bread and reset the timer.

"Bread's ready," she called over. "Want some?"

"Of course, I do. I'm over here starving," I teased.

She fetched two small plates out of a cabinet before crossing over with the bread. As she handed me one of those plates, her fingertips brushed mine, and it felt as if sparks shot from that glancing contact. Although I was being perfectly honest when I told her Thea would be pissed if I expected Jane to make other arrangements, I was doubting the wisdom of having her stay here. My reaction to her was powerful and confusing. If needed, I could always change my own plans. Truthfully, though, I really wanted the time here. I craved being far removed from my life.

A while later, we had finished eating and put the leftovers away. Jane turned toward me in the archway of the kitchen, sliding her hands into her back pockets. That motion had the unintended effect of pushing her breasts forward and stretching her long-sleeve T-shirt across them.

"Thanks for not telling me I had to leave. It looks like we're going to get plenty of snow from this storm," she commented.

"No doubt," I replied as I glanced out the windows.

"Well, I'm going to go to bed. I'll see you in the morning."

It felt as if tension was vibrating on a string between us. I willed myself to keep my demeanor cool. "That you will."

Her lips curled in a quick smile as she turned and headed down the hallway. I stood by the windows and stared out into the swirling snow, wondering again if it was a mistake for me to stay. I went to sleep not much later, deciding I would figure it out tomorrow. The end of the snowstorm and a little sunshine might help me think more clearly.

Chapter Three

JANE

"So much for sunshine," I muttered to myself as I looked out my bedroom window at the blowing snow. This storm was a genuine nor'easter and hadn't let up, not even a little, during the night.

Turning, I crossed over to the dresser and picked up my phone. I tapped the screen and pulled up my weather app. Today's forecast predicted twelve inches of snow and potentially more. Tomorrow's forecast was for even more snow.

Fuck. I'd had a restless night of sleep with the wind waking me several times and my awareness of Ian through the bedroom wall adjacent to the room I'd claimed keeping me keyed up.

I knew I could stay here, but my body's fierce reaction to him was annoying. It rubbed me the wrong way that he didn't even remember who I was at first. It brought up all those old feelings from high school—feeling out of place, the nerdy girl. It wasn't as if high school had been awful. It had simply been frustrating, almost an obstacle to get through.

Ian had been chased after by plenty of girls. Not

only had he been handsome and funny and popular, but he'd actually been sort of nice.

I sighed to myself. I didn't even know if I wanted to attempt to drive over to my parents' old home. It had been boarded up for years, and the power and water were turned off. There was no heat. My plan had been to stay here and have a month to myself, but now Ian was here. His mere presence was interfering with my plans.

"Crap," I muttered.

The lights flickered when the wind gusted, and I let out a breath of relief when they stayed on. I decided it'd be wise for me to take a shower while we still had power.

I grabbed my toiletry bag and a change of clothes and found myself peering down the hallway when I stepped out. This was one of those old colonial homes —two stories with bedrooms flanking a wide hallway upstairs and one bathroom. Ian had claimed the room beside mine, the master bedroom, which probably had a bathroom.

Tiptoeing into the hall bathroom, I flicked the lights on and looked around, my lips curling in a smile. The room had tiny tiles in a checkered design of black and white. I was relieved to find a stack of towels in a cabinet beside the shower because I hadn't even thought to check with Thea about bedding and towels.

I eyed the bathroom door for a moment before I stripped out of my clothes. It still didn't lock, and I laughed to myself, recalling how the broken lock annoyed Thea when I spent the night over here because she had to share the bathroom with her brothers. I figured Ian would hear the shower, and my need for a shower overrode my caution. Before my drive up yesterday, I'd had a tension-filled day. I hadn't started my new job yet, and I was still tying up loose ends at my old job. One of those loose ends involved my nightmare of a former boss who couldn't finish a single project without me and several of my colleagues doing most of the work for him. He was a complete asshole.

I shoved those worries away and climbed into the shower. I was quick because I was mindful that if we lost power, the water might turn off. Only minutes later, I was toweling off, and the fan was still running. The old ceiling fan was the reason I didn't hear the door open.

"Right, I'll call in next week. But when I said I was taking a vacation, I meant it." Ian was talking on the phone, not even paying attention to the fact that I was in the bathroom.

I squeaked in surprise, and his head whipped in my direction. I had been leaning over, scrubbing the towel over my hair. I flung my hair back and yanked my towel up, but I was pretty sure I wasn't quick enough to prevent him from seeing me completely naked.

"What are you doing?" I burst out as I tightened the towel around me.

He said into his phone, "I need to go. We'll talk when I'm available."

Mind you, the door was still wide open and all I had to cover me was a towel, which felt more than insubstantial.

He lowered the phone, tapping his thumb on the screen to end the call. We stared at each other for a moment as I scrambled to find my composure.

"Could you please leave?" I managed, annoyed that my voice sounded squeaky.

His gaze was cool as his eyes held mine. His lips quirked at the corners. "The master bath is being renovated, so this is the only usable bathroom upstairs. Maybe you should've locked the door."

Oh. My. God. He was still in here. In this tiny bathroom. With me. My nipples tightened.

"The lock doesn't work," I ground out. "Now, could you please leave?"

"Yes, ma'am," he drawled.

I didn't like the teasing tone in his voice, and I bristled all over. I was also hot and prickly and beyond frustrated. He didn't hurry out either, only adding to my overall state of fluster. He stepped back slowly, dipping his head once more as I clutched the towel to my chest. I waited until the door clicked shut. Then I scurried across the bathroom, the tiles cool under my feet. I stood right in front of the door as if prepared to prevent him from coming in again.

I listened through the doorway, only to hear his low chuckle before he added, "My apologies. I was on the phone, and I was distracted."

My breath was shallow, and I had to take several deep breaths just to get enough air in my lungs. I tried to order my pulse to stand down.

I dressed in record time. I hadn't planned on wearing a turtleneck, but I opted for one after my little encounter with Ian. I felt the need to cover as much as possible. I walked downstairs, telling myself I would be cool and calm and collected when I saw him in the kitchen or wherever the hell he was.

The scent of coffee carried down the hallway. As soon as I stepped into the kitchen, I said, "I hope you made enough for both of us." My tone came out sharp, bristling with my annoyance.

So much for playing it cool. Whatever. Ian had apparently showered in the downstairs bathroom. His hair was damp, and his skin slightly flushed. He glanced over, his gaze calm and cool. "Of course, I did. I'm not an asshole, even if I did accidentally walk in on you. My apologies again."

"It's okay," I said stiffly. "I didn't mean to be rude just now."

He shrugged. "No problem. I'll try to fix the lock today."

"Thanks," I murmured. I looked out the window, feeling the heat burn on my cheeks and willing it away.

"How do you like your coffee?" he asked.

"Do we even have any cream?" I turned toward him.

He flashed a quick grin, then pointed at the counter. My eyes followed and landed on a small box with those little cream containers. "The date hasn't expired. Someone must've gotten them recently. Noah and Sasha were here last month."

"Well, that's handy. I'll take a little cream."

"We have sugar too," he offered, gesturing toward a small container sitting beside the cream.

"I don't like my coffee sweet, but thanks."

He filled a mug for me and set it beside the box of creamers. I added two to the coffee and crossed over to sit at the kitchen table. Snow swirled outside, and I couldn't even see the ocean.

"According to the weather, the snow is going to last all day and probably into tomorrow," I commented.

"I know," Ian said as he sat down across from me. He held two creamers in hand and poured them in before lightly swirling the mug in his hand and taking a swallow. He set it down, adding, "I called down to Haven's Bay Grocery. They're open. I'm thinking of heading in."

"You are?"

"I have an SUV with four-wheel drive. It shouldn't

be too bad, and the drive's not very far. What were your plans for today?"

"I was going to go investigate my parents' house."

"I'm not sure it's worth it in this weather."

That comment pricked me. "I thought I'd check to see if it was worth me trying to stay there."

Ian's eyes narrowed as he shook his head. "No."

"No?" I countered. "I'm pretty sure you don't get to tell me what to do."

"I don't think it's a great idea in the weather."

"If you can drive to town, so can I," I protested, feeling downright contrary.

"Jane, you're not going to stay there. There's no power or water. You cannot stay there," he said, *way* too firmly for me.

I knew what he said was entirely logical, but still. I bristled and straightened in my chair, narrowing my eyes at him. "That'll be my decision. Once the storm passes, I'll go take a look and see what I want to do."

His brows arched up. "I'll go with you."

"You're not my keeper," I retorted.

"No, but you're a friend of Thea's, so by extension, a friend of mine. Your parents would kill me if I let you try to stay there."

I felt that pesky flush creep up my neck and into my cheeks again, and before I could even think of what to say next, other than to volley back and forth in this sort-of argument, he added, "Do you want to go to the grocery store with me?"

I shrugged.

"How long were you planning to stay?"

"Until Christmas. I'm reconsidering that plan," I replied. I honestly didn't know if I could take too many days, much less a few weeks, in this house with

Ian. My hormones were annoying the hell out of me, and this big house seemed too small for both of us.

"No need to do so on my account," he responded smoothly. "I already checked with Thea. She told me your lease in Boston doesn't start until January. Were you going to spend Christmas with your parents?"

Sweet Jesus. This man was driving me crazy with his questions.

"No."

One of Ian's dark brows rose in a slash. Back in high school, he'd had this easy confidence, the kind of casual confidence most guys tried to emulate. But Ian actually had it. Now, a decade later, it was honed even more sharply. The mere rise of a brow felt imperious. I took a swallow of my coffee, trying to ignore the little hum of awareness in my body. I did *not* want to notice Ian. For one, that was ridiculous. He was my friend's older brother too. He didn't even recognize who I was at first. Talk about feeling stupid and too familiar with the keen awareness I wasn't worthy of recognition.

I didn't think I looked that different from when I was in high school. I didn't really *have* to explain anything to Ian, but I did anyway. "My parents' anniversary is near Christmas, and they've always wanted to go to Paris, so that's where they're spending their anniversary this year. With me moving and starting a new job, it wasn't a good time for me to travel. So, no, I'm not spending the holiday with my parents."

He nodded. "Makes sense."

"What about you? What are your Christmas plans?" I countered, figuring I might as well be nosy about him.

Chapter Four

IAN

Jane pressed her glasses up her nose, her hazel eyes holding mine as she waited. I was still trying to recover from seeing her in the bathroom. Fuck me. Jane Matthews was delectable, sexy, and tempting beyond belief.

Just now, even though I knew I shouldn't be remembering it, my mind conjured up the recollection of seeing her bare. Her skin flushed and pink from her shower, her lush breasts bouncing slightly when she'd straightened, and her nipples a deep, dusky pink and pebbled from the contrast of the cold air to the heat from the shower. She'd yanked that towel up fast, but not fast enough to prevent my brain from searing her image into my memory.

I gave myself a mental shake, ordering my focus to the present. Of course, she still looked delectable with her honey-blond hair drying in tousled waves around her shoulders. Atop her jeans, she wore a turtleneck sweater, completely covering the top of her. Of course, that only made matters worse for the state of my libido. It felt like a challenge. I knew what lay underneath now, and she had hidden it so thoroughly, all I wanted to do was make her notice me as much as I noticed her.

Jane cleared her throat. Pursing her lips, she eyed me over the rim of her coffee cup. "Well?" she prompted.

"Well, what?" I countered, having completely forgotten her question. So much for keeping my focus on track.

"What about you? How long are you planning to stay here? What are your holiday plans? That sort of thing." She circled her free hand in the air before taking a swallow of coffee.

She had a great mouth. I didn't need to be lingering on it, but I did. Her lips were pink, her bottom one fuller. I could just imagine the soft give of them underneath mine. She blinked at me, clearing her throat again.

Right, I needed to get with it. "Well, I was planning to stay here until Christmas as well."

"What are your brothers planning? Are they coming up here? Thea wasn't sure."

"I don't think so. Dallas has a new baby, and Noah's wife, Sasha, is pregnant and due soon."

"Oh, that's so great!" Jane smiled, pressing her palm to her chest. "I'm really happy to hear that for him and Sasha. I haven't seen Sasha in years."

"They live in Boston now too," I offered.

"I know. It'll be nice to reconnect with her."

Jane's eyes dipped down for a moment before she looked up. "So, how come you're taking a whole month off from work?"

Ah, that was the awkward question I didn't want

to answer. Not honestly, that is. "I just really need a vacation," I said, which was entirely true. It's just I was also skirting the reasons behind why.

I worked a lot, and for the most part, I liked my job. In a way, I felt as if I were trying to make up for everything my father did wrong. My father had also worked in investments, but it all blew up when Dallas, my eldest brother who worked for the FBI, had stumbled across my father's connection to a large fraud operation involving money laundering. Dallas had handed off the case, but the result was our father sitting in jail. Our mother had passed away before that.

I had hoped to go into the family business, but instead, I struck out on my own, doing my damnedest to rebuild our family's shaky financial situation. I could never fix what my father did, but at least I could try to repair the damage. There was no glory in it, but I prided myself on building investments in socially responsible areas. Both of my brothers worked in the FBI. Noah had followed Dallas into the field while Thea was a lawyer and worked for a large firm.

All three of them were living in Boston now. I was still in DC, seriously reconsidering what I wanted to do. I was up to my eyeballs in evidence because I was a whistleblower in an investment consortium, but I couldn't tell Jane about any of that. The investigators down there had recommended I take a break. I knew I needed the break, but I didn't really know how to take a vacation because I hadn't had one in years. I sure as hell hadn't expected to be sharing the house with Jane. Not that I minded. Maybe she could be a distraction. We could certainly argue. She was primed for that.

I finally shrugged, adding, "I've worked a lot for

too many years. I figured some time on the snowy coast of Maine would be a complete change of pace from investments and politics."

Jane nodded slowly. "You never wanted to go into the FBI like your brothers?"

I shook my head sharply. "Hell, no. Are you kidding? That job is seriously stressful."

"True. I was just curious because both of your brothers do it."

"I know, and they love it, but it's not for me. I'm not as serious of a guy." I remembered Jane being very serious in high school.

"No, you never were," she said, her lips twisting slightly, which annoyed me.

"What do you mean?"

"Just that you were a sports star, the class tease, the guy who all the girls chased. That's what I mean."

"Nobody chased me." Irritation flashed through me.

Jane looked at me over the top of her glasses. For a second, it felt like a stern school teacher was looking at me.

I stared back at her and finally shrugged. "I'll own the class tease thing, but I wasn't a player or a jerk. Did I do something to offend you back then?"

Her pretty eyes skated over my face, assessing me before she took another swallow of her coffee and shook her head. "On second thought, I'll pass on the grocery store." She didn't say anything further.

For some reason, I annoyed Jane, and I wanted to know why. I also thought she was cute. *Really* cute. Deliciously, temptingly cute. I'd expected to come up to Haven's Bay and bang around this big old house by myself. I'd even imagined doing a little ice fishing. My main goal was to forget the troubles I'd left behind in

Washington, DC. I'd even worried I might be a little bored. But with Jane here, there was no way I'd be bored.

She was a challenge, and I thrived on rising to any challenge.

Chapter Five

JANE

After Ian left to go grocery shopping, I peered outside. The snow had slowed to plump flakes floating down from the sky. He'd somehow arranged for someone to plow the driveway. That made up my mind. I knew the roads would be plowed. Maybe it had been a while since I'd lived through a full Maine winter, but I could certainly handle a drive in this weather. It wasn't sunny or clear, but I had good winter tires. I didn't want to stay cooped up in the house by myself.

Although I felt like I could breathe a little easier once he left, it was impossible not to be aware of him. I was beyond annoyed with myself that I was so drawn to him. The awareness was an almost constant prickle over my skin. All of Thea's brothers were handsome, but only Ian had gotten to me when I was younger. Oh, I hadn't really crushed on him. I'd always been too guarded to let myself crush on anyone. Although I had to admit he was cute. Because he was. Even though he was too handsome for his own good, he was nice then and even nicer now.

For a flash, I wanted to lie to myself and pretend he'd been a jerk, but he never had. "He just never really noticed me," I muttered to myself.

I felt like I was crushing on him now. And *that* was fucking ridiculous. I gave my head a shake. I hadn't told Ian, but I planned to go check out my parents' house. Maybe it would be easier to get the power and water turned on than I'd thought.

He'd even asked me about my grocery preference, and I'd brushed him off, telling him not to worry about me. He'd eyed me curiously. I figured he was going to stock up anyway because he was that kind of guy, and apparently, he felt some sort of responsibility to me or to Thea on my behalf. Whatever. I couldn't spend my mental energy on what Ian thought. That fell into the category of ridiculous.

I slipped into my down jacket and my winter boots, which I had wisely packed, and started my car. I scraped the ice off my windshield while the engine warmed. Whoever had plowed the drive had done a good job. I only had to shovel a little bit of snow away from the front of my car.

A few minutes later, I was driving through Haven's Bay. I couldn't help but smile at the picturesque little town. Even on a snowy day, shoppers were out in the downtown area. The festive holiday decorations glimmered through the lightly falling snow. I was tempted to stop in at a few shops, but I decided against it. Perusing the shops could wait for a better day.

Only minutes later, I slowed to turn off the main road onto the street that would lead to my parents' house, my old childhood home. They had moved away after I finished high school. For a while, they used the home during the summer. But a few years back, my father had a stroke. He had recovered well, but the stairs were a challenge for him. They'd emptied the house out and buttoned it up while they decided what to do. They'd finally opted to put it on the market. I was tasked with checking on the house, getting rid of any last boxes that were still here, and making sure it was ready to be put on the market.

The pace of the snow had started to pick up again, but I felt like I had my snow driving skills back up to speed. I was handling the roads like a champ until I turned into my parents' driveway and promptly bumped into something solid. That bump sent me off track in the unplowed driveway, and I bounced into a tree on the opposite side of the drive.

The car came to a jolting stop. "Fuck," I muttered.

My pulse had lunged ahead when I lost control. After a moment, it slowed as I realized I was merely listing to the side of the driveway. I thought I might as well see if I could back up. Putting my car in reverse, I lightly feathered the gas pedal. The tires spun on the snow. It was only then I realized I didn't even have Ian's phone number. I had Thea's, and I could always call a car service place.

"Dammit." I rested my forehead against the steering wheel.

I was relieved it was early in the day, so I had plenty of time to solve my little problem. I was certain I just needed someone to pull me out of the deep snow, and I would be on my way again.

I decided against calling Thea. I knew that meant she would call Ian, and my pride wasn't ready to deal with the I-told-you-so from him. I called the car service that came with my insurance. The friendly lady on the other end of the phone told me she would see who she could get there and gave me an ETA of an hour.

"Okay, thank you," I said through my gritted teeth.

I'd had the foresight last night to stop and get gas at the last service station on the highway before I took the exit for Haven's Bay, so I could wait an hour or more if needed in my heated car. I had my phone, so I could even read a book. I tapped open my reading app but discovered I was too distracted to focus on the plot.

Turning on the radio, I listened to the news, but I made the mistake of checking my email and narrowed my eyes when I saw yet another email from my now former boss. I sighed. Apparently, he wanted more help with the last paper. I had no idea how that man ever got tenure, but then wasn't that the way of the world? Hapless men succeeding from the effort of the women who did the behind-the-scenes work.

I took a deep breath, and my fingers hovered over my phone screen as I considered replying. After a moment, I had the sense to close my email and lower my phone. I actually did *not* work for him anymore. I smiled to myself. I didn't even need to reply.

The car service texted me to tell me someone could be there in the promised hour, but no sooner because they were dealing with several other calls that had come in sooner. The news rambled along as I waited. Perhaps a half an hour had passed when I heard a sound behind me.

I turned in my car seat to look around and saw a vehicle behind me. "Oh, awesome! They're here early."

It wasn't a tow truck, though. It was an SUV, but maybe they were just checking on me to see what I needed. I clambered out, walking through the knee-deep snow to find Ian glaring at me as he stepped out of the SUV.

"What the hell are you doing?" he opened with.

"What the hell are *you* doing?" I lobbed right back at him.

"When I got back to the house and realized you'd been crazy enough to leave in this weather, I figured you came here. I knew the driveway wasn't plowed, and as far as I can tell, you're stuck."

I rolled my eyes. "It's fine. Not a big deal. I've already called a car service."

Ian muttered something under his breath. The snowfall had let up yet again, so I had a clear view of his eye roll. "You're coming with me."

"I'm not coming with you. I'll wait for the car service." I crossed my arms.

"Fine. Then I'll wait with you."

"Oh my god, you're kidding me," I muttered. "Don't you need to drop the groceries off?"

"I already have," he ground out. "Let's wait in my SUV."

Determined to out-contrary him, I retorted, "No, I'll wait in my car."

"Fine, I'll sit with you in your car."

"What if I don't want you to sit with me in my car? Oh my god, you're such a man!" I exclaimed as he walked through the snow, stopping in front of me.

"I *am* a man, so it only stands to reason I am such a man."

"You know what I mean. I wasn't making that comment as a factual statement."

He shrugged. Just then—hallelujah—the car service showed up early. "Oh look, they're already here. I don't need you to wait. I'm sure they can get my car out, and I'll drive back myself."

I glanced longingly over my shoulder at my parents' long driveway that was blanketed in snow and the dark house that sat at the end. The energy I'd summoned to figure out how to get the utilities turned on blew away with a gust of wind. Ian waited with me as the car service guy got out. As soon as he got closer, I recognized him. "Joe!"

Joe Martinelli smiled over at me. "Well, hey, Jane. How's it going?"

I eyed my car and shrugged as I glanced back at him. "Minus my car being stuck, I'm fine."

Joe grinned. "I'll help with your car." His eyes shifted to Ian, and for a second, there was a thread of tension. Joe was Thea's only boyfriend in high school. Her father had refused to let them continue dating, and she'd been heartbroken over it. Joe's family owned the town's only automotive repair place, and her father had considered him beneath her. I had no idea if Ian had an opinion on any of that.

He cast an easy smile. "Hey, Joe, good to see you."

Joe dipped his head. "Same here. How's life?" We chatted briefly before he asked, "How's Thea?" His tone was casual, but we all knew the question was loaded. Joe and Thea had been high school sweethearts until her father forbid her from seeing him.

Ian replied, "She's pretty good. I'm sure she'd love to catch up."

"Maybe sometime," Joe said lightly, and that was that. He shifted his attention to my car.

Moments later, Ian had moved his SUV. Joe hooked up the tow truck and pulled my car back to the center of the snow-covered drive.

He got out and did a quick circle around my car before looking over at me and shaking his head. "What's wrong?" I asked.

"Your tire rim is bent," he explained.

"What does that mean?" I said, ignoring the sinking sensation in my stomach.

"You need a whole new rim and the tire to go with it. You can't drive on it now."

"Are you kidding?" I muttered as I rounded my car.

Ian was right behind me and peered down at the tire in question on the front passenger side. "Definitely not driving this. It also looks like your oil pan got torn off."

Joe chimed in, "There are boulders on the corners of this drive. Granite is very unforgiving. I'm guessing you couldn't see them in the snow and probably caught your oil pan on it when you bounced to the other side of the drive. You don't have to book with our shop, but you can."

"What are we talking about money-wise?"

His eyes darted over to the stain in the snow, that I only noticed now, and then back to me. He lifted one shoulder in a shrug. "I'm not sure. I need to get a look under there, and I'm not going to get a good look in this snow. For now, do you want me to tow it to the shop, and you can decide what you want to do?"

I sighed, trudging around to the passenger side to fetch my purse. "That's fine," I called. "And of course you can do it. What kind of timeframe are we looking at?"

"Probably a week or two. We're pretty busy. If you need it sooner, I'm sure I can try to squeeze it in, but it really depends on if I need to order parts."

I bit back another sigh because I didn't mean to sound ungrateful, and this wasn't Joe's fault. "That's fine. Should I give you a credit card now?"

He grinned and shook his head. "No, just call the shop. Give me your phone number, and I'll give you my card. I'm running the emergency service today, so I won't even be in the office much. Good to see you. What are you both doing here?" he asked us as he hooked my car up again and slowly pulled it onto the flatbed.

"I'm taking the month off before I start a new job in Boston. Turns out Ian's here too," I explained.

"Oh, did you come up together?" he asked as he raised the flatbed to level and tightened the chains around my tires.

I shook my head quickly, and Ian chuckled. "Clearly, that's a no," Ian offered. "If you were wondering, Jane's not pleased that Thea forgot to tell me I wasn't supposed to be staying in our family's home right now."

I rolled my eyes. "It's not a problem." I glared at Ian when Joe turned away.

After Joe was ready to go, he assured me once his shop had time to look at my car, they would call with an update on how long the repairs would take.

I climbed into the passenger seat of Ian's SUV, my eyes taking it in. It was nice, very nice. It was all black, which suited his personality. The seats were leather and heated. I couldn't even hold back the hum of appreciation at the feel of the warmth that immediately seeped through me.

Once I was buckled in and the door was closed, Ian's eyes slid sideways, his mouth kicking up at one corner. My belly startled me with a somersault, and I felt tingles spreading all over. Jesus, this was so annoying. I was getting turned on just from him sort of smiling. Needing a distraction, any distraction, I commented, "These heated seats are nice."

His grin widened. "I love them." He adjusted the heat, asking, "You warm enough?"

"I will be soon. No need to turn it up."

He waited while Joe backed the tow truck out, and I watched my car moving away. He put the SUV into reverse, commenting as he backed up, "Next time you get a new car, maybe look into heated seats. They're more standard than they used to be."

"I'll keep that in mind."

Once he was on the road, we rode in silence for a few minutes. I wrestled with the tension humming through my system—a combustible mix of annoyance with Ian's high-handedness, the situation with my car feeding into it, and this persistent attraction to him.

"How're you doing over there?" Ian's question broke through the quiet.

"Fine. I'm a little frustrated about my car," I admitted.

"It doesn't seem like a huge issue. In the meantime, obviously, I can drive you wherever you need to go."

I bit my bottom lip, trying to keep a sigh from slipping out. Now, I was here without a car and dependent on Ian unless I decided to rent one. Considering that I didn't have tons of money saved up, I preferred not to incur that cost. I managed a light shrug. "Thanks for that. Hopefully, the shop can take care of it pretty quickly. At least I don't have many places to go. I don't want to impose on you."

"You're not imposing. It's not like I have a ton of things to do. I can't imagine you're going to treat me like your own personal driving service," he teased.

I laughed softly. "No, I won't. When the weather's better, if you could take me over to check out my parents' house, that would be great. Otherwise, I just need to take care of food and things."

"What was your plan for your time here anyway?" he asked.

I looked out the window of the SUV, watching the snowy landscape roll by. "Aside from taking out any last boxes at my parents' house, I didn't have any plans. I wanted a break and some peace and quiet."

"How about you?"

"Peace and quiet is my plan. Things have been tense at work, and a break was in order." He slowed to turn onto the main road that led through town.

"I hope me being here doesn't interfere with that." It felt as if we were on a loop of similar conversations, anything to break the tension.

"It won't," Ian said confidently.

It frustrated me that I was annoyed because his presence *did* interfere with my peace and quiet. I felt unsettled, and my old feelings of insecurity from high school were rising to the surface. High school was such a crappy time in life, not only for me but also for many people. Ian was like that example of everything I wasn't in high school—confident, easygoing, carrying his popularity with comfort.

I had gone on to college and gotten my master's and my Ph.D. I felt successful and had confidence in myself. Yet there was one small thing I wanted to change. I hadn't dated much. At all. And inconveniently, I was still a virgin. It wasn't because I was uptight or prudish, but I had prioritized other things in college and graduate school, and now here I was, feeling too old.

I couldn't say precisely why, but Ian's mere presence triggered that insecurity in a major way. Probably because I knew the man had likely played the field his entire adult life. Because he could. When Thea and I had gotten together for coffee the day before I drove up here, we'd caught up on personal news. She joked about Ian, saying he was the last brother not to fall in love with Dallas and Noah both married. Thea was bitter about dating and told me she'd sworn off men.

She'd laughed about Ian, saying he refused to consider anything that wasn't casual.

He was the very kind of man who chafed on my nerves. The fact that my body thought he was *all* that and then some was incredibly annoying.

Forcing my thoughts off my body's reaction to Ian, I commented, "Downtown is as cute as ever."

He slowed when he approached the town green, the typical center of town park-type area ubiquitous throughout New England. A Christmas tree stood in the center of the green with its lights glittering through the still falling snow.

"Haven's Bay is a cute town," he agreed. "Sometimes, I forget how quaint it is."

"Do you like living in the city?" I asked.

He came to a stop at a light and glanced over. When his green eyes met mine, a little shiver chased down my spine, and I felt my cheeks flushing.

"Sometimes, I like it. Sometimes, I don't," he replied.

"Oh," I managed in response.

The light changed, and he looked forward again. When I caught my eyes noticing his graceful yet masculine hands curled around the steering wheel, I forced my gaze away. I unconsciously took a deep breath. I didn't realize I'd let it out in an audible sigh until Ian asked, "You okay over there?"

Chapter Six

IAN

I heard the sound of Jane's breath drawing in sharply and felt her attention whipping toward me. I slid my gaze sideways. Her eyes were narrowed, and her cheeks a little flushed.

"I'm fine," she said, her tone sharp.

"Well, that was a sigh over there." I looked forward again. I didn't know why, but I enjoyed needling Jane.

"I was *breathing*," she sputtered.

"Of course, you were breathing, but that was a heavy sigh. You sounded annoyed."

She let out a huff. "Well, *now* I'm annoyed. Obviously, at you."

I chuckled. "What did I do? I'm not the one who tried to drive down a snow-covered driveway and hit a boulder. I told you it wasn't a good idea."

"Oh, my God," she muttered. "I've been driving on winter roads for years. I grew up here, for God's sake. I didn't think about the boulders marking the end of the driveway. So yes, if you want to give me a little hell about that, go right ahead." She swept her hand through the air.

I bit back the urge to laugh again. "Can you give me the name of whoever plows your driveway?" she asked. "I'll call them to have them go over to my parents' place."

"I'll call," I offered.

"I can call," Jane insisted.

"Jane, it's a friend. I'll take care of it. They might be booked up, but they'll fit it in for me." I didn't want to say out loud that I'd already made the arrangements for her.

She let out another belabored sigh. "Oh my god, are you kidding?"

"No, I'm not kidding. I'll take care of it."

I could practically feel her bristling. "Could you please just give me the information?" Before I could respond, she added, "You know what? Don't even bother. I'll find someone myself."

Oh, great. Now, I'd have to tell her I'd already dealt with it. "No point. I already called them. It'll be taken care of once the storm is over."

"Well, how much are they charging? I need to pay for it."

"No, you don't," I ground out. "I'll take care of it."

"Oh, my god. You are really bossy."

"Maybe so, but I don't really care."

Jane mumbled something under her breath. This time, I chuckled aloud.

When we got back to the house, Jane promptly went up to the bedroom she'd claimed. That was fine with me. I put away the groceries that I'd left on the counter in a hurry. After that, I

began working on a project I'd started during my last visit here. Between my brothers and I, we were gradually getting this house back in order. This house and the property it sat on were the only assets that had survived the aftermath of my father's fraud case. The furniture had been sold off, along with just about everything else. We'd used the proceeds to reimburse losses for those affected by the fraud.

The house had sat empty for several years, and it had been old, to begin with, so I had plenty of things to work on. We'd replaced the boiler last year. I'd set out to gradually update the windows and sills and redo the cabinets in the kitchen. With it being winter, I didn't want to do any painting, but I'd basically turned the rec room downstairs into a workshop, so I'd started cutting the trim for the numerous windows in this house. This project would probably take me two or three years, depending on how often I could travel up here.

I didn't mind. It gave me something to focus on and was a complete shift from what I usually did, which was to bury my head in numbers and deal with investment decisions. For the past six months, I'd been smack in the middle of the whistleblower case. It was hard to ignore the tension about that and even more difficult to ignore my laptop and emails. I'd actually disconnected my email accounts on my phone, which was a smart move because then I couldn't easily check them.

After a few hours of work, I got hungry and went into the kitchen to make a sandwich. I was surprised to see Jane there, peering into the refrigerator. I stopped in the archway, hesitating to enter the room. It didn't help that Jane was leaning over, and I had an excellent view of the sweet curves of her hips. She'd changed out of her jeans into a pair of comfortable sweatpants with these giant wool socks on her feet. The cotton outlined her bottom delectably.

Fuck me. Of all the things I had planned on,

getting the hots for one of my little sister's old high school friends wasn't one of them. That said, I relished the distraction she offered.

Walking into the kitchen, I commented, "I got plenty of food for both of us."

Jane squeaked. Straightening and spinning around, she closed the refrigerator.

"Didn't mean to startle you," I offered.

She lowered her hands, and a lovely pink flush washed over her cheeks. "What are you doing?"

"Coming to get something to eat. What are you doing?"

She shrugged. "Same." She pressed her glasses up her nose. "Sorry I was a little bitchy earlier."

"Oh, I don't mind. I kind of like you bitchy. We can argue, and that's fun."

She pressed her lips in a line and blinked at me behind her glasses. "Seriously, Ian? How old are you?"

"Thirty-two, last time I checked," I said dryly.

She crossed her arms, oblivious to the fact that doing so plumped up the tops of her breasts. I could see the lush curves along the edge of her V-neck T-shirt. "I do recall you being like this before. That's why I said you were the class tease."

"Did I tease you?" I asked as I walked over and opened the refrigerator, pulling out bread, sandwich meats, and cheeses. I was a sucker for good cheese and had gotten an excellent selection, if I did say so myself.

"No, you didn't tease me. You didn't really notice me," she replied.

"I doubt that. I noticed you."

"Ian, you didn't even recognize me at first."

"It *has* been over ten years. Cut me a little slack."

Jane's mouth twisted, and she rolled her eyes. A

pleasant hum of electricity chased through me when I saw the flush rise on her cheeks.

"I basically look the same, ten years or not," she protested.

I fetched a knife out of the silverware drawer and cut off a piece of cheese. Turning toward her, I shook my head. "No, you don't. You were serious and hardly looked at me. Now, you're fucking sexy with a whole librarian vibe."

Her eyes went wide, and her breath drew in sharply. This time, her cheeks flushed a deep red. I was enjoying this *way* too much. "I do not—" she sputtered and then shook her head before shrugging and casting me a sheepish smile. "Okay, I definitely wasn't sexy in high school."

"You were also my sister's friend. I tried *really* hard not to pay attention to Thea's friends."

"Really?" Jane countered. "Is that a thing?"

"I don't know what you mean by 'a thing,' but it was for me. It was kind of a respect thing, I guess. You were also a few years younger than me, which is the equivalent of a decade in high school."

"The younger students are basically invisible to the upperclassmen," she commented.

Her eyes slid to the cheese as I moved to cut another slice. "Would you like some?"

"I would, actually." Her stomach growled just then, and she slapped her hand over it.

I chuckled. "Take your pick." Gesturing to the array of cheeses on the counter, I handed her the knife.

"You don't mess around with cheese."

"I *love* cheese."

She flashed me a grin, and a sizzle of heat jolted through me. "Same here. Which isn't great."

"Why isn't that great? Cheese *is* great."

Jane gestured toward her hips with her free hand. I dipped my eyes down, not even bothering to hide my lingering look of appreciation.

"If you're implying that cheese causes a weight issue, you do *not* need to change anything," I said bluntly.

She didn't reply and cut herself a healthy slice of cheese. "When's the last time you came to Haven's Bay?" she asked, shifting the topic.

"Just a few months ago. I came up this fall. Ever since we started working on the house, I make time to come up and do a few projects whenever I can. My main thing right now is replacing all the windowsills."

She was chewing, but her eyes went wide. She swallowed and cleared her throat before replying, "This house has a lot of windows."

I grinned as I stepped to the counter. She handed me the knife, and I opened several more packages of the cheeses. "It does, but they're all old and need to be replaced."

"Do you know when this house was built?"

"Late 1700s."

"So it's over two hundred years old," she observed.

"We still have the original windowsills."

"It's amazing they've held up this long."

I chuckled. "Yeah, and there's probably an inch of paint on them, but it's time for new ones. I'm working on the inside of the sills during the winter, and I'll take care of the outside when it's nice."

"You're replacing the windows too?"

I nodded. "It won't be cheap, but we're all working on it together, so it'll work out." I leaned my hips against the counter as I took another bite of cheese.

"Have you spent much time in town on your visits up here?"

Jane took another piece of cheese, resting her hips on the counter beside me. "Oh yeah, Emile's and Bay Bistro are still delicious. We should grab dinner soon. Maybe tonight." I glanced out the window. "The snow is supposed to let up in the next hour or two."

Jane's gaze followed mine to look out the window. The snow was nothing more than flakes floating from the sky, and patches of blue were opening up amongst the thick cloud cover.

She looked back at me. "Dinner?"

"Yes. You know, the meal that you have in the evening so you don't starve during the night?"

She eyed me dubiously.

"Come on. Emile's has upped their game. They serve locally sourced foods and more."

Her eyes blinked at me from behind her glasses. She swallowed and caught the corner of her bottom lip with her teeth, worrying it just enough to send a jolt of awareness through my body. She finally shrugged. "Okay. We can have dinner, but it's not a date," she clarified.

"No? Why not?" I couldn't help but tease. "We are having dinner together, and we're staying here alone at the house together."

Jane's eyes narrowed. "It's *not* a date."

"What if I want it to be?" I didn't know why I was pushing this issue, but I was. More than anything, I enjoyed getting a rise out of her.

Her nostrils flared when she let out a forceful breath. "Seriously? I'm definitely not the kind of woman you would ask on a date anyway, so why pretend? I'm just your sister's friend. Don't try to make it something it's not."

Her comments irritated me. "You have no idea what kind of woman I would ask out on a date," I countered.

She turned away from me, pushing off the counter and stepping to the sink. She rinsed her hands under the water, replying as she turned to face me while she dried her hands on the towel. "Back in high school, you were into cheerleaders."

I tried to remember who I dated in high school, but in all honesty, I hadn't been serious about anyone. I didn't like admitting it, but Jane was right. I had dated more than one cheerleader. In college, I didn't date any cheerleaders, but I did date a few pretty, popular girls. I felt a twinge of discomfort because Jane was beautiful now in a way that went much deeper than the surface. Maybe I hadn't noticed her in high school, but she was beautiful then too.

She'd just kept to herself and was quiet. Whenever she was here hanging out with Thea, she was more relaxed. Not that I spent time with them because, well, Thea *was* my younger sister. We were just close enough in age that we often argued, even if we loved each other.

"Does high school really define who we are later on?" I mused.

Jane lifted one of her shoulders in a shrug. "No, it doesn't. But coming back to Haven's Bay brings back all those memories."

"That makes sense." A part of me wanted to keep pressing, to rile her again, but I sensed now wasn't the time and that this was a more sensitive topic for her than me. I glanced at my watch. "So, dinner around six? I'll drive."

She let out a dry laugh. "Of course, you will. I don't have a car."

I winked. "No, you don't. You'll have to rely on me."

"Are you going to hold this over my head?" She turned and hung the dish towel over the handle of the stove.

"Nope. I'm just glad it turned out I was here."

"What do you mean?"

"If I wasn't, you'd be without a car," I pointed out.

"I would have just rented one," she snapped.

"Right, because there's a car rental place here in Haven's Bay," I deadpanned.

Jane actually stuck her tongue out at me at that, and I laughed. She waved over her shoulder as she walked out of the kitchen. "I'll see you at six. I have a little work to do," she called.

Chapter Seven

JANE

I stood in front of the mirror in the bathroom, staring at my reflection. I ran my hands through my hair and adjusted my glasses. This was *not* a date, so worrying about my appearance was ridiculous. I reached into my toiletry bag and snagged my lip gloss. I silently insisted to myself, as I carefully swiped it across my lips, that I would wear lip gloss out to have dinner with a friend, which was true.

Liar.

My cheeks got hot. When I looked one last time and noticed my glasses, I let out a sigh. Contacts had never worked for me because I had astigmatism in both eyes. It made contacts annoying, at least for me. So what if I wore glasses? I didn't care.

I hadn't cared for years, but somehow Ian's presence triggered something in me. I didn't want to claim he *made* me care, but he elicited old insecurities about how I looked and how I'd always wanted to be invisible in high school. It had felt like being caught in a crosscurrent—wanting no one to notice me and wishing I could be popular at the same time.

"Stop being stupid," I muttered to myself.

I tucked the lip gloss in the pocket of my jeans and turned to leave the bathroom. I felt the heat rise to my cheeks again as I opened the door and heard the subtle snick of the lock. Ian had fixed the lock on this door, but it was impossible to forget he'd seen me bare naked. As I returned to the bedroom, I stopped once again, looking at myself in the mirror mounted on the back of the door. I was wearing fitted jeans with a pair of leather boots. It was winter, and I needed to be practical. Atop that, I wore a silky camisole with a soft cashmere cardigan that buttoned halfway up. It was warm and stylish.

I let out another sigh. Because, apparently, thinking about my appearance and having dinner with Ian drew a plethora of sighs. I almost couldn't admit to myself what I was thinking. Maybe Ian could help me take care of a small problem. I felt the buzz of attraction between us, and I didn't expect it to go anywhere or mean anything. But he was experienced, and I was decidedly not. I was no prim and proper girl. I'd had boyfriends in college, but I'd never gotten to the final act, and I still carried that tag of virgin silently inside. I didn't even tell my friends about it because they all assumed I'd made it beyond that milestone.

Trust was a weird thing for me. High school hadn't been easy. I had enough sense now to know it wasn't really easy for anyone, even the popular kids. The social environment was unforgiving in more ways than one. But then I'd gone on to college, and the guy I'd liked the most and just thought I might let down my guard with had ended up falling for my roommate. I didn't even think I could say anything about it. That was how things were in college. We weren't serious yet, and she was cuter and bubblier than me.

For the remainder of college, my sex life had been limited to kisses and foreplay. After that, graduate school had swamped me in work. I jumped from there to even more work. I was young in my field and trying to climb the career ladder, so I didn't have time for dating. I didn't meet many people outside of work, and having a fling or even dating a coworker was out of the question because I needed to keep the respect of my colleagues.

Heat climbed up my neck and into my cheeks—again. I was going to proposition Ian and suggest he help me solve my problem. I'd probably never see him again even though I'd moved back to Boston. According to Thea, he was so busy with work she rarely saw him. It was perfect. I trusted him. I knew not to have any romantic expectations, and I would finally rid myself of that pesky issue.

I grabbed my purse and left my room, the heels of my boots echoing on the hardwood floor as I walked through the hallway and down the stairs. Ian was waiting by the door. He didn't look up right away, and I paused, glancing down. He had his phone in his hand and was looking at something. His dark hair caught glints from the chandelier in the entryway. One foot was crossed over the other at the ankles as he slouched casually against the wall. He wasn't doing much of anything, yet he was still so fucking sexy.

My eyes traveled over his muscled shoulders, the dark hair dusting his forearms and up to the clean lines of his features. My belly did a shimmy and a flip. I started walking down the stairs, and his gaze lifted. When our eyes caught, my belly did another flip. He pushed away from the wall, sliding his phone into the inside pocket of his jacket. He was silent as I stepped off the bottom stair and crossed over to reach for my jacket hanging on the coat rack.

"My SUV's warming up," he commented.

The mere sound of his voice sent a shiver down my spine. Turning, I nodded and hoped my cheeks weren't too pink. "Good. I hate getting into a cold car. I forgot about that this morning before I left."

His teeth flashed with his smile. "I suppose it's not that cold out in Seattle."

I slipped into my jacket. "It's rainy, but the winters definitely aren't like they are here. I imagine they're not too cold in DC either."

"Definitely not." He held the door for me.

I felt his presence behind me as he closed and locked it. I didn't know what to think when he paused by his SUV and opened the passenger door for me. "Thank you," I murmured.

He simply dipped his chin in acknowledgment as he closed the door, waiting until I buckled my seat belt.

Moments later, he was driving through the early evening. The snow had finally stopped, and stars were glittering in the darkness through the passing clouds. I looked out the window, watching as we passed by homes with holiday lights twinkling. "It feels so familiar," I whispered, not even meaning to speak aloud.

"It does, doesn't it? It's weird how you can be gone for so long and come back, and the feeling snaps into place."

I glanced toward him, and my breath hitched in my throat. His wrist was resting on the edge of the steering wheel with his hand dangling. Something was so simple and confident about the flexion of his forearm as he steered around a small curve in the road. His profile in the dim lights from outside was etched in shadow. The stark cheekbones, his strong, square jaw.

Ian was familiar to me too, yet this feeling he produced wasn't. Not at all. Back in high school, he'd been Thea's annoying older brother. Of course, I thought he was handsome. Just like all the girls, well, except for Thea. Back then, his presence and popularity poked at my insecurities too sharply.

"How long were you away before you came back?" I heard myself asking.

His eyes slid sideways, catching mine. The collision felt like metal striking pavement as sparks flew in the air between us.

"Years." He looked back to the road, shifting his hand onto the steering wheel and appearing to count with his fingers. "Five."

"What was that like for you?" I asked, referencing the skid of their father into fraud and jail after their mother passed away. Somehow, I knew I didn't need to clarify.

His gaze flicked to mine again as he came to a stop. "Strange. Things were really stressful as I'm sure you heard from Thea."

"I heard a little. She didn't talk about it much."

He looked back toward the road, the sound of his blinker loud in the SUV as he turned. "I suppose she wouldn't. None of us did. It was difficult and embarrassing. I'm just grateful our mom wasn't here then. I miss her, and I wish she was still here, but that would have been devastating for her."

My heart twisted with a sharp ache. While I'd rarely seen their father in the time I spent with Thea, I knew he'd been cold and distant. But their mother had been warm and kind and everything you'd want in a mother.

"It would have. I'm sure you miss your mother."

Ian didn't look at me, but it felt as if a gust of desolation passed through him.

"I loved your mom. She was awesome," I said softly.

He cast me a quick smile, the warmth in his eyes evident. "She was. She passed on, and a few years later, all that stuff went down with our dad. What a mess."

We were quiet for a few minutes as he drove. I recalled the news stories about their father. Dallas and Noah both worked for the FBI. Dallas had been investigating financial irregularities in some high-end investment companies, but he'd had to remove himself from the case when he realized their father was involved. As a result, their family had lost just about everything. According to Thea, Ian had worked hard to repay everything their father had owed. Meanwhile, Dallas sold off most of their family's assets to contribute, saving only the old family home.

"I'm sorry," I offered quietly.

I felt his shrug, catching the tail end of his shoulder lifting when I glanced over. "Thank you. We're fine."

"Do you talk to your father?" My question surprised me, but I was curious.

"Occasionally. He was an asshole before."

He paused, and I tried to think of the right thing to say, landing only on, "I'm sorry."

He let out a sharp breath. "Enough of this depressing conversation. I had an awesome mom and have three amazing siblings. My dad's a criminal and an asshole. Could've been worse."

"It's good to count your blessings when you can," I said lightly.

"Tell me about you. Your parents are well, I hope?"

I nodded. "They're retired and finally ready to sell the home here. They both have a few health issues. My father's stroke limited his mobility, but otherwise, he's pretty good."

"He's okay?" Ian prompted, his tone sincere, reminding me he was a legitimately nice guy.

"He is. It's nothing they can't manage."

"So, your job is to come up here and get the house ready for the market?"

"That's the plan. They still have some things stored here. Well, not really stored, just never moved."

"It's a good location. Real estate values are strong these days."

I made a noise of agreement and looked out the window as we lapsed into quiet. Silence didn't feel uncomfortable with him, except for the fact that I couldn't seem to quell my body's awareness of him.

His presence was too potent, but it was more than that. He was handsome and sexy, and there was this underlying vibration. He exuded this easy confidence with a hint of arrogance, which should have annoyed me but didn't. Restless, I shifted my legs, crossing and uncrossing them before lacing my fingers together in my lap a little too tightly.

"So, they've updated the menu at Emile's?" I asked because I had to say something.

It wasn't the silence that was getting to me. It was the subtle vibration circling through my body. The air felt weighted with a charge about to go off.

"Sherry and Emile still work there but not as much. One of their daughters went to culinary school and revamped the whole thing when she came back.

They have the old favorites and a lot of new high-end stuff. She usually has good specials. They do the whole farm-to-table thing during the growing season."

I felt my lips curling into a smile. "I'm glad Sherry and Emile are still here and doing well."

"I'm pretty sure they'll both live forever," Ian offered with a confident nod as we approached the town green.

Haven's Bay was a typical New England town. The town had been built around the green when it was established a few centuries ago. The rectangular park in the middle of downtown had shops lining all four sides of it with houses mingled amongst them.

Ian slowed, his blinker loud again inside his SUV as we approached Emile's. Sherry and Emile owned this restaurant, along with the main grocery store in town and a few other businesses. They were quite wealthy, although you wouldn't know it. They lived in the very home they'd inherited from Emile's parents. They were one of the many longtime French-Canadian families who lived in Maine.

"Oh, they've even renovated the building," I commented as he parked toward the back.

"I called in a reservation," he offered with a quick glance sideways.

"Is that necessary?"

His low chuckle sent a wash of heat through me and a shiver over my skin. "It's popular now. Not only for locals but also tourists."

Ian climbed out of the SUV and rounded to the passenger side in a flash, opening the door before I had even unbuckled my seat belt. "Did you run around the front of your SUV?" I teased.

His half-grin sent my belly into somersaults. A moment later, our footsteps crunched on the gravel parking lot. He held the door for me at the entrance. With his hand resting on my lower back as he coaxed me through, I could feel the heat of his palm sifting through the fabric of my clothing. I shouldn't like that touch so much, but I savored it. He was a gentleman, always polite, always gracious. I was a little startled to discover that just about everything he did spun into the heat sliding through me.

The moment we walked in, I began to doubt my plan. As soon as we entered the reception area, a woman I recognized, Shelly Chambers, stood from a bench, where she was sitting with a man I didn't recognize. "Oh, my gosh! Ian Tate!" she exclaimed.

Shelly was one of those very cheerleaders who I was pretty sure Ian had dated. He didn't seem as excited to see her and dipped his chin in acknowledgment. "Well, hey there, Shelly. How are you?"

"I'm great." She looked at me, and I knew she recognized me. I absolutely *knew* it, but she cocked her head to the side, casting a quizzical look in my direction. "And you are?"

Ian interjected, "Jane Matthews. You remember her, right?"

He slid his arm around my waist, his hand curling just above my hip bone. I could feel the heat of his touch again, almost possessive. I had no idea what to think of how he was handling this.

I watched as Shelly's eyes dipped down. I could feel her trying to calculate and assess who we were to each other. I smiled tightly. "We were in high school together. I think I tutored you in math."

Okay, maybe that was a shitty thing to say. Shelly wasn't stupid. She just didn't try in school because she'd had other matters on her mind. She gave me a bright smile. Everything about her felt as plastic now as it did then, and I hated how insecure I felt. She was still beautiful. She had cornflower blond hair pulled up in a lovely twist. She turned, gesturing toward the man sitting on the bench. "This is my husband, Todd."

The man smiled at us politely but said nothing. "Well, it's good to see you," Ian said when the receptionist looked up. He kept his arm around my waist and led me toward the desk.

"Jane Matthews!" Sherry Levesque said as she rounded the desk, her face breaking into a wide smile.

"Hi, Sherry. It's good to see you."

She pulled me into a warm hug, stepping back and glancing at Ian. "You didn't tell me this is who you were bringing to dinner with you." Her lips pressed in a line as she cast him a teasing but disapproving look.

"I didn't even talk to you when I called to make the reservation, Sherry," Ian protested.

Sherry grinned warmly at him. "But I know everything."

"That's right. I should've known someone would tell you I made a reservation."

Sherry turned her attention back to me. "How long are you here?"

"A month," I offered. "I'm getting my parents' house ready to sell."

"Your parents' house doesn't even have power. Please tell me you're not trying to stay there," Sherry said with a tsk.

Before I could respond, she glanced at the receptionist, who nodded and called over that our table was ready.

"I'll walk you over."

Sherry picked up menus as Ian replied before I could, "Of course, Jane's not staying there. She's staying at our house."

"Oh, so you're both there. Well, isn't that nice? Now, are your brothers and Thea joining you soon?" Sherry asked while she led us across the restaurant.

"I'm not sure. We might be doing Christmas in Boston," Ian responded.

"Well, don't you dare leave Jane alone. Your parents are going to Paris, aren't they?"

Of course, Sherry would know that. "How do you still know everything?" I asked as she stopped at a table by the windows and pulled out a chair for me.

Her eyes twinkled with her sly grin. "I just do. Actually, your mother does call a few times a year to check in. She let me know you'd be up here. Please give her a hug for me the next time you see her. I understand why they're selling, but I'll miss seeing them."

"I'm sure you will," I offered.

"If I ever retire, I'll visit all my old friends," she commented.

Ian rolled his eyes as he sat down. "I can't imagine you retiring, Sherry."

"I don't work as much as I used to, young man. My daughter runs this whole place. I just show up and occasionally act like I'm working," she teased.

At that moment, someone called her name. "Speaking of. She must need me for something. I love to feel needed. Make sure to get something good, and if you need anything, just wave me down. I'll come help."

"I'm sure we'll be fine. It's good to see you, Sherry," I replied.

"Oh, don't worry, dear. You'll see me again." She hurried off, and I spread a cloth napkin on my lap and opened the menu.

This setting felt downright romantic, which didn't

fit with my plans. The last time I'd been here, this restaurant had more of a casual family vibe. Now, it felt elegant. Candles sat atop the tables, and the crisp white cloth napkins matched the tablecloths. Everything had been renovated. The hardwood floors gleamed under the dim lighting, and the low hum of voices surrounded us.

Proposing to Ian that he take care of my virginity like it was a business matter in a casual restaurant had seemed easier than this. I did *not* want to lend a romantic vibe to it.

I told myself it was just the setting, nothing more. Lifting my eyes to his, I looked away quickly, scanning the space. "They must have shut down to do these renovations."

"I know. I wasn't here when they happened, but I heard they did."

Even the worn old wide-plank flooring had been refinished to a glossy sheen. Before, the wall that faced Haven's Bay had one or two windows. Now, the entire wall was windows, and it felt as if we were seated on the edge of the ocean. The moonlight shimmered on the water, the surface rippling under the lingering breeze from the snowstorm that had passed hours earlier.

"It's really nice," I said when my eyes finally made their way back to his. I forced myself to hold his gaze and not shy away like a nervous pony. "Good call to make reservations," I added. Seeing as the restaurant was at capacity, we'd have had to wait without them.

His teeth flashed with his grin. "I like to plan."

"So, Shelly must still live in town then," I commented, immediately berating myself for mentioning her. There was no point.

"I wouldn't know. Haven't seen her in years, probably not since high school."

"Do you stay in touch?" There I went, being curious again.

He arched a brow, his look sardonic. "No. If I did, I would know if she lived in town."

I felt my lips purse and was instantly annoyed with myself. I didn't need to scold him. "Didn't you date her in high school?"

As soon as I asked that question, I berated myself. That question was born from my insecurities.

Ian shook his head. "I did not. Should I ask who you dated in high school?" he countered pointedly.

"No, because I didn't date anyone," I snapped.

His piercing eyes searched mine, and I shifted my legs uncomfortably, but I didn't break away. "You had your priorities straight."

"What do you mean?"

"Guys are kind of dumb in high school. You realize after the fact that other things are more important than having fun."

"You seem like you're doing all right, and I think you had fun in high school," I offered.

Our conversation paused when a server arrived. I ordered a glass of red wine because I needed to calm the hell down and take the edge off my nerves. Ian ordered a scotch. The server reeled off a list of specials and then handed us the menus. After he left, Ian glanced over at me, commenting, "I didn't catch all of that."

"Me neither, but everything sounded good."

He chuckled. "Everything is good."

We perused our menus, and I settled on my order quickly. I couldn't resist one of the specials—sauteed scallops with a maple glaze, risotto, and seared vegetables.

Ian surprised me when he picked up the thread of our conversation. "I didn't have my priorities straight. As you recall, our dad was an asshole, and he was worse with my brothers and me than with Thea. School was an escape for me, and I liked having fun because it was the only thing that made life bearable. I had to scramble afterward. My grades had been so-so, and I didn't want to work for my dad. I knew I wanted to go into finance."

"You knew that right off?" I prompted.

"It probably wasn't for the best reason," he offered, his gaze self-deprecating. "I wanted to one-up my dad and show him I could do it without him. I got my MBA after working my ass off at a mediocre college. It turned out to be a good thing I went into finance because that's what helped me scramble things together for the rest of us after we lost pretty much everything but the house." His tone was dry and matter-of-fact.

"That must've been hard."

"In the end, money really doesn't matter. I definitely learned that," he commented with a shrug.

"Do you like working in finance now?"

Something passed through his gaze then, and I wanted to grab on to it, to understand it, but it was gone as fast as it appeared. "Yes and no. The older I get, the more cynical I get."

Chapter Eight

IAN

Jane's hair caught glints of light from above and from the candle on the table between us. I shifted in my chair. I was the one who had invited her to come to dinner with me, and I was doubting it was a good idea. I kept telling myself this was no date, yet it felt like one.

Emile's was the kind of place for a romantic evening. I wouldn't think anything of it if I weren't nearly tied up in knots with need for her. I'd been thinking about her comment off and on, about how I never noticed her when we were younger. I wanted to say it wasn't true, but it was.

It had been easy not to notice her. She was one of my younger sister's friends, so that sort of automatically made her off-limits. But she also wasn't the kind of girl I paid attention to back then. I'd been looking for nothing more than a good time with any girl who might give it to me. All I wanted was fun.

Jane was smart and on the bookish side. Seeing her now, I discovered I had a librarian fantasy I never knew existed. With her glasses and when she pursed her lips and looked at me kind of like a schoolteacher, it was all I could do not to whistle through my teeth and tug her onto my lap.

So, there I sat, my cock so hard it ached. My jeans felt uncomfortably tight as I shifted in my chair. I wanted the brush of her fingers over my cock, not mine. As I tried to distract myself and adjust myself once again, Jane was saying something, and I lost the thread of the conversation. She stopped talking completely.

"Are you even listening to me?" She pursed her lips again, sending a sizzling jolt of lust straight to my balls.

"Of course." That was a total lie, but I would try to wiggle out of this one.

"What was I talking about?"

A wink and a quick smile were not going to dissuade Jane. "Well, I asked you about work, and you were telling me about your job out in Seattle. Something about your boss."

"What about my boss?"

"You thought he was awesome," I quipped.

Jane rolled her eyes and lifted her wine glass, taking the last swallow. When she set it down, her tongue swiped across her bottom lip. Now my cock ached even more. I tore my eyes away from her mouth, looking down at her fingertips where she idly traced the stem of the glass.

"I hated my boss. He was an asshole who relied on everybody else to do his work for him, and then he took the credit. Now, could you please just admit you weren't paying attention? I prefer that to you trying to tease me into thinking otherwise."

Her eyes held mine steadily. I finally cast her a

sheepish smile. "Fine. I lost track of what you were saying, but I have a good excuse."

She tipped her head to the side, lifting her hand away from the wine glass to catch a lock of hair that had fallen loose. She spun it around her finger, and I watched it slide in quick circles. She cleared her throat. "What's your good excuse? I can't wait to hear it."

"You're distracting," I said flatly, my voice almost coming out in a growl.

Her hand stilled and dropped to her lap. She straightened, her eyes blinking behind her glasses. I'd surprised her and felt like I'd caught my balance for the moment. Jane had me feeling off-balance almost every moment since we'd ended up in Haven's Bay together.

"I'm distracting?" she prompted, her tone laced with doubt.

"You're beautiful," I replied, deciding honesty was my best course here.

Her cheeks went pink. She closed her eyes for a moment before opening them again. "Flattery doesn't change the fact that you weren't listening. Try again."

"Oh no, I'm telling the truth. You don't understand just how distracting you are."

Leaning forward, I reached for her hand where it had fallen on the table. I curled mine over it, trailing my thumb across the silky skin on the inside of her wrist. I could feel the rapid beat of her pulse there and watched when her lips parted slightly as she took in a sharp intake of air.

"What? No one else has told you you're beautiful? I'm going to guess, if that's actually the case, it's because you've mastered the art of brushing guys off."

Pink crested higher on her cheeks, her flush deepening when she bit the corner of her lip. Fuck me. I was already in bad enough shape. As it was, my zipper was going to permanently imprint on my cock if I had to tolerate much more of this.

"What do you mean?" she asked.

"Just that. I get it. Maybe I didn't notice you in high school, and maybe other guys didn't notice you in high school, but high school is weird. You kept to yourself. You're brilliant, and you're a professor now, so that's probably a little intimidating to some men. That's no excuse because men can be total idiots. You also hold yourself back. I can guarantee that. When's the last time you dated someone?"

Jane's eyes widened slightly, and regrettably, she released her bottom lip. Then she slid her tongue across it again as if to smooth over where she'd been worrying it with her teeth. I needed to kiss it. That would make it all better.

She shrugged lightly. "Sometime last year."

I could practically see her brain clicking into gear. Her gaze turned assessing, and I felt her pulse lunge on the inside of her wrist. I waited. I was good at waiting people out.

"I have a proposition," she said, her voice a little raspy.

"Oh, this ought to be good. A proposition?"

She nodded. Her blush deepened. She was wearing this silky camisole with a soft cashmere sweater that buttoned a little low. I could see the shadowed valley between her breasts, and the teasing hint of her curves. I wanted to peel that sweater apart to see all of her.

"You're probably going to think I'm crazy."

I shrugged. "I doubt it. Aren't we all a little crazy?"

Her lashes swept down, and I watched as her

shoulders rose and fell with a deep, shuddering breath. When she opened her eyes again, she lifted her chin slightly and squared her shoulders. "I need a favor."

"Anything."

"I'm a virgin, and I would prefer not to be because it makes things awkward for dating. People take it seriously, like it's this big deal. It's not to me, but I'd rather not worry about it. It seems like it would be sensible to deal with it with someone I know. We're here for a couple of weeks. Just once, and then you'll probably never see me again after this. It won't be complicated."

So much for finding my balance in this interaction. I felt as if Jane had kicked my feet out from under me, and I'd fallen to my knees. All I could do was stare at her. I didn't even realize my mouth had fallen open until she said, "You can close your mouth. It's not that weird. I'm not that old. See? This reaction of yours is exactly why it's a problem. Guys freak out. I know some guys are really into that whole first thing, but I'm not up for being someone's trophy like that. I don't even want to have this conversation anymore because you look all shocked." She waved dismissively at me.

I felt caught in two opposing riptides. My need for Jane had just exploded. I'd never cared one way or another about someone's level of experience, but the idea that I could be her first? Holy hell.

The other riptide was no fucking way. This was my sister's friend. There was a reason I had carefully ignored all of Thea's friends in high school. There were blurred boundaries and complications, all kinds of things I just didn't want to deal with. My life was stressful enough right now.

It wasn't even possible to contemplate getting into

a relationship, not to mention that I hadn't ever been interested in a relationship. Even though that wasn't what Jane was asking, there was no way I could just use her like that. While I sat there scrambling to find my footing again, Jane let out a sigh and tugged her hand away from mine.

"You're freaking out. I bet you're thinking you don't want to use me, or it should be someone else. I don't want anything serious, but I also don't want it to be some guy from a dating app who gets off on the whole virgin thing." She released an annoyed sigh, her lips pressed in a peevish line. She leaned back in her chair and drummed her fingertips on the table.

"Could you speak?" she prompted dryly.

"Jane, that's—"

She circled her hand in the air when I couldn't get past those words. I didn't even know what to say.

"I don't think that's a good idea," I finally said.

"Why?" Her tone was sharp.

"Because you're Thea's friend."

She rolled her eyes. "I'm almost thirty years old. It's not like I'm some high school girl. I knew I shouldn't have said anything." She narrowed her eyes and actually pointed her finger toward me. "Don't you dare tell anyone what I just told you. Thea doesn't know."

"Of course not. I wouldn't say anything to anyone even if you hadn't asked."

"Back in college when I should've been dating and just having fun, I was focused on other things. Now, it's turned into this, well, this *thing*. I just want to deal with it. Maybe look at it like a project, like I need you to help me fix something on my car."

I ran a hand through my hair, more frazzled than I wanted to admit. "You're not fixing a car or putting in a new window. You're a person. I can't..." I ran my hand through my hair again, giving up on trying to find my way out of this conversation. I finally shrugged. "I don't know how to explain it."

For a split second, I could've sworn I saw hurt flickering in her eyes, but she looked away, lifting her water glass and taking a swallow. "Fine, but now you see my point."

I thought maybe we could get out of this insane conversation. The problem was I wanted Jane—fiercely. And I didn't know what to make of any of this. Sherry stopped by and chatted with us for a few minutes. All the while, I was hyperaware of every subtle move Jane made. I heard the slide of her silky camisole when she adjusted it. I heard the motion of denim when she crossed her legs. It felt as if something had fallen around us, a shimmering net filled with sparks colliding against each other and multiplying the heat factor by thousands. I was accustomed to feeling in control, especially with women, yet this entire evening had spiraled well out of my control.

After Sherry left, Jane spoke again, "I shouldn't have brought that up. I didn't mean to make you uncomfortable."

"There's no need to apologize," I replied, trying to keep my tone level and casual to keep my mind off imagining what she would feel like beneath me.

"I must have misread something," she added.

"Huh?" That was how much my conversational skills had devolved.

"I thought there might be some chemistry between us, so it might be something you wanted. I should've known better." Her dry tone was almost self-deprecating.

I didn't like that, not at all. "You didn't misread anything," I insisted.

Jane rolled her eyes. "Clearly, I did. You looked shocked for a few minutes there. Don't worry. It's no big deal."

The server brought our check, and we almost got into an argument over who was paying. Jane finally gave in when I told her that Thea would give me hell if I let Jane pay for dinner.

We drove home, the entire ride silent. My cock still ached, and I was torn over what to do. My good angel told me to respect Jane.

Don't take her up on this crazy proposition because it is crazy. She's a virgin, but she's a nice woman. She deserves to be with a man who can give her something serious.

I'd never had a single serious relationship in my life, nor had I even contemplated one.

When we got back to the house, Jane practically ran up the stairs and waited impatiently at the door. After we stepped inside and she moved to hang up her coat, I went and said something stupid. "You were wrong."

"About what?"

"Misreading the situation. A part of the problem is I want you. Too much."

Her head whipped up. She had just hung her jacket on the coat rack beside mine. I noticed the way her nipples pressed against her silk camisole. It was chilly in the foyer. It always had been.

When I saw the doubt flickering in her eyes, I did the next stupid thing. She was standing right in front of the door with her back to it. I took two strides, closing that distance between us. She took a step back, her breath hitching in her throat when she collided with the door.

"What are you doing?" she whispered.

"This."

Although desire was running hot in me—at this point, it was lava in my veins—I forced myself not to rush this. I might be sane enough not to be the one to take her first time from her, but I would give her a kiss and make sure she knew she hadn't misread anything. I just wasn't the right guy for her. I wasn't the right guy for anyone. Not right now.

Lifting a hand, I reached up and caught the thin tie she used to hold up the twist in her hair. As soon as I pulled it out, her hair fell in a glossy tumble around her shoulders. I let my hands slide through the locks. Moving slowly, I gave her a chance to tell me to back the fuck off. I dipped my head and dropped a kiss at one corner of her mouth and then the other. I felt the whisper of her breath when she let out the barest whimper. Then I brushed my lips across hers, before finally angling her head to the side and claiming her mouth.

She might not be mine, but at this moment, her mouth was. As soon as our lips met, it felt as if lightning sizzled through my body. She let out another whimper, and her tongue darted out to glide against mine. I lost control of that kiss in a blazing hot second. My control was like a leaf falling into a bonfire and burning to ash.

I was devouring her mouth, taking deep sips of her. She was warm and sweet, and I could taste the plummy tones of wine on her tongue. By the time I came up for air, I was plastered against her. I hadn't even realized I'd hooked my free hand under her knee and lifted it as I rocked my arousal into the cradle of her hips. The sound of our ragged breathing echoed in the foyer.

I was stunned. I dragged my eyes open. Her gaze met mine, heavy-lidded and dark. Before I could form a thought, I was kissing her again. Because it was the *only* thing to do. My hands were greedy, sliding up to cup her breasts, my thumb rubbing over her nipple through the silk. I growled into her mouth when she arched into me, rocking her hips against the hard ridge of my arousal.

My good angel finally broke through the haze of need and raw lust clouding my mind. I tore my mouth free of hers again, leaning my head back to gulp in air.

"Now, do you see?" I asked when I leveled my eyes with hers again.

She blinked and nodded. I honestly didn't know how I did it, but somehow, I untangled myself from her and stepped back. She remained leaning against the door, her palms flat against it. She stared at me with her lips kiss-bitten, her cheeks flushed and her eyes hazed with desire.

It was *all* I could fucking do not to lift her into my arms, carry her upstairs, and fuck her for hours. Because I didn't know if I would ever get Jane out of my system. And that was the crux of the problem.

For the second time tonight, she left me speechless. When I realized I didn't know what to say, I simply turned and went upstairs, walking straight into the bathroom to take an ice-cold shower. Despite my painfully aroused state, I resisted the urge to take care of matters in the shower, telling myself this need would pass. It was no use. I woke up in the darkness later and ended up finding my release with my hand. It was nothing compared to what I knew it would feel like if I was buried inside Jane. I'd lost my fucking mind over that kiss.

Chapter Nine

IAN

The following morning, I woke in the darkness. Instantly, Jane sashayed into my thoughts. I was so annoyed with how much I could *not* stop thinking about her that I kicked the covers off and stalked into the bathroom.

After another cold shower, I walked downstairs quietly and started coffee. When I flicked on the outdoor light that illuminated the area outside the kitchen, snow was falling heavily.

"Looks like we're in for another snowstorm," I murmured to myself.

I pulled up the weather app on my phone, confirming what I already knew. We had another nor'easter coming in. It would be snowing all day.

I groaned aloud and tossed my phone on the counter. I'd be bouncing around this house with Jane. I needed to get busy. That was the only way to stay sane. I didn't need to be thinking about her virginity and her absolutely ridiculous request.

"Jesus fucking Christ," I muttered to myself as I got coffee ready and tapped the start button.

It wasn't even six in the morning. I didn't know when Jane would be awake. I didn't know her routine. She'd been up before me yesterday, but I'd been exhausted, and I hadn't been up most of the night with my mind spinning over the replay of our kiss. I didn't usually make mistakes, not with women.

Even before the blowup at work, I didn't have time for romance. I had a few casual relationships where I occasionally saw someone and had dinner to get things out of my system. It didn't interfere with work and didn't interfere with my peace of mind. Jane *definitely* interfered with my peace of mind. I shook my head as I left the kitchen and walked into the area I'd set up for work. I had a stack of trim lumber in the corner and quickly scooped up the notepad where I had jotted down the measurements for the different rooms. For the most part, the windows were uniformly sized. However, there were some exceptions as this was an old house.

We had some small windows for decorative purposes. I decided to focus on cutting the trim for those. That would give me something to do for most of the day, and I'd manage to stay out of Jane's way. It would also keep me from giving in to the urge to check my work email.

I returned to the kitchen to discover the coffee was ready. I was pouring myself a cup when I heard the sound of the water turning on above the kitchen. Fuck, that meant Jane was already awake. Apparently, she was an early riser too. Just fucking great.

I bitterly wished she'd had as restless of a night as I had. Maybe she thought she could keep things uncomplicated between us, but I knew that kiss had been hot for her. Her responsiveness was part of my problem.

There was a pure quality to her ardor. It was the way she threw herself into the kiss.

Forcibly kicking those thoughts away, I filled my cup of coffee and toasted a bagel. An empty stomach would only make me more irritable, and my baseline mood wasn't that good to start with today. Only minutes later, I heard Jane's footsteps on the stairs as I was smearing cream cheese on the bagel.

I reflexively turned as I heard her enter the kitchen. Her hair was damp, the honey gold darkened. Her cheeks were flushed and pink from the steamy shower. My entire body revved like a race car engine at the sight of her. Her fleece leggings hugged her shapely hips and was paired with a loose fluffy sweater with a V-neck. I instantly recalled the feel of her nipple, the taut peak under my touch. I forcibly nudged my thoughts off that track and cleared my throat.

"Good morning, you're up early," I commented.

She pressed her finger on the center of her glasses, pushing them up on her nose slightly. "So are you. Good morning."

"There's enough coffee for you," I offered, gesturing toward the coffeepot.

"Thank you," she said politely.

The tension between us felt thick, only adding to the heavy desire flooding my body. I willed my arousal to dissipate. I did *not* need to be acting like a randy teenager around her.

"You're welcome to have a bagel too. Looks like we're in for another snowstorm today."

That was safe. We could discuss the weather and food, and maybe I'd forget her insane proposition last night. Insane and wildly tempting.

"I'm going to work on cutting the trim for the windows," I added.

Jane stopped beside the coffeepot, opening the cabinet above and pulling out a mug. She glanced toward me and then at the windows. "Oh, it's already snowing. I didn't even check the weather this morning."

"We'll probably get another foot. I'm glad we have plenty of groceries for now."

She nodded. "Thank you again for getting groceries."

"Of course. We both need to eat." Nothing like stating the obvious to try to kill my distraction at her presence.

She filled her coffee cup, her cheeks tinged with a wash of pink as she watched the dark liquid pouring. "We do," she agreed. "What kind of cream cheese did you get?"

I felt my lips curling into a grin. "The good kind. Smoked Atlantic salmon. That's a special at Haven's Bay Grocery. I got a few other options too."

"I forgot how much I loved their cream cheese selection," she offered with a smile.

"I forgot they even had one."

"I think they were ahead of their time on that," she said as she crossed to the refrigerator, opening it and getting out the cream.

"I think so, but Sherry loves to cook, so she's always making something."

Jane poured cream in her coffee and then got out a bagel. "How did you sleep?" she asked politely.

Because I was feeling contrary, I decided to be honest. "Not well."

"Oh." She looked a little taken aback. "I'm sorry."

"That's okay. It's your fault."

She had been lifting her mug to her lips and lowered it as her eyes narrowed. "How is it my fault?"

"Your little proposition."

"I have no idea what that has to do with your sleep," she said pointedly.

Because I'd apparently lost my mind, I crossed over to her, setting my mug on the counter, and leaned forward. "How did you sleep?"

Pink crested on her cheeks, and she caught the corner of her bottom lip with her teeth. It felt like a whip cracked through the air, the sound sizzling down my spine and going straight to my balls.

She shrugged and lifted her chin. "Okay," she rasped.

Her blush deepened. "You're lying. Let me tell you how I slept. I couldn't stop thinking about you after your proposition. I came all over my hand thinking about it, and I'm already hard for you again."

Jane's breath drew in sharply, and her eyes widened. She shifted on her feet as she whispered, "Oh." The sound of her swallowing was audible in the quiet room.

A gust of wind blew against the house, rattling the windows. It felt as if the storm itself was mirroring the state of my body.

"Am I supposed to apologize?" she finally asked before clearing her throat.

I shook my head slowly, sanity somehow rising through the depths of my need for her. I shackled myself and stepped back, lifting my coffee cup again. "No, that's not necessary."

I knew it was rude, but I turned and left the room without another word. I could hardly stand to be near her. All I wanted was her, and I needed to get a fucking grip.

Chapter Ten

JANE

I stood in the kitchen, listening to Ian's footsteps retreating. My pulse scattered wildly, and my breath was short. I could feel the arousal slick at my core and shifted my thighs to relieve the ache building there.

Ian was right. I *had* been lying about last night. I'd hardly slept at all, tossing and turning as my body hummed with unquenched need. I'd found myself dipping my fingers into my slippery wet and swollen folds and bringing myself to a rapid orgasm. That had barely taken the edge off. And now? I was already hot and bothered. All over again.

Restless, I turned and walked to the windows at the back of the kitchen. The snow was picking up its pace with the wind blowing from the ocean toward the house. The old house shuddered against the force. I took a deep breath, hoping my pulse would slow. I didn't know what I was going to do with myself, and I didn't know how to take back what I'd done. I felt so stupid about telling him the truth.

Now, he knew a secret I'd kept from pretty much everyone. I sighed and turned away from the windows, deciding I might as well work. My new job didn't officially start for a few weeks, as far as the campus, but I had access to the university's online system, and I could set up my syllabus and all that. I needed something to do, or I was going to lose my mind.

Chapter Eleven

IAN

I was grateful to have some kind of project that required attention to detail. The necessity of accurate measurements and getting the cuts just right for the windowsills and trim succeeded in mostly getting my mind off Jane. However, my body knew she was in the vicinity.

Knowing she and I were the only two people here kept a subtle thrum of awareness and arousal vibrating in my body. I finished most of the trim for the non-standard-sized windows and decided it was time for a lunch break. After sweeping the sawdust off the floor, my cell phone rang. When I glanced at the screen, I was surprised to see it was my office assistant.

It was still snowing. I was still here in this house with Jane. This distraction would be better than none, so I answered.

"Hi there, Marilyn."

"Hi, Ian. How are things in Maine?" she asked.

"They're good. It's snowing again."

I could hear her smile as she replied, "It's Maine, and it's winter. Did you expect anything else?"

I chuckled. "No, I suppose not. Anyway, to what do I owe the pleasure of your call?"

She paused, just long enough that I knew she was worried. Marilyn was my one and only assistant, and I trusted her completely. She was incredibly efficient and had her fingers on every detail. She was one of the very few people who knew what I was dealing with.

"I thought I should give you a heads-up that Tom Daniels called over trying to schedule a meeting with you."

I took a breath, letting it out with a sigh. "Really?"

"Of course, really," Marilyn replied tartly. "It may mean nothing."

"It doesn't mean nothing, Marilyn. Tom rarely schedules meetings with me. Have I gotten any more calls from the investigator's office?"

"No, and they said they'll call you directly if something is urgent. I did call over there and let them know he reached out to you."

"Good. Thank you."

"How worried should we be?" Marilyn asked after another long pause.

"You and I will be fine, Marilyn. It's just an ugly situation."

Her sigh filtered through the phone line. "It is. Why do people have to be so greedy?"

I chuckled again. "Well, if you didn't want to ponder that question, you shouldn't have taken a position as my assistant. I work in finance. Just about everyone who works in finance is greedy."

"You're not," she countered.

"Now, that's where you're wrong. I may not cheat and steal and lie, but I went into finance to make money."

I could practically envision her pursing her lips and

glaring at me. "Why yes, anyone who works in this field is trying to make money. But it's possible to want to make money and do well without being a greedy asshole."

"Good point," I returned. "Let me know if you hear anything else from Tom. What did you tell him?"

"The truth. That you're out of town and will be until after the holidays."

"Do you think he accepted that?"

"Well, it's true, so if he checks on it, that's what he'll find."

"Another good point," I returned. "Keep me posted."

"You know I will. If I don't talk to you before Christmas, Merry Christmas."

"You'll talk to me before Christmas, Marilyn."

"How do you know?" she teased lightly.

"Because I'll call you and check in and make sure you and Dan have an excellent Christmas basket," I said, referring to her husband.

I could imagine her rolling her eyes at this point. I was generous with my holiday office gifts. "That's not necessary, you know."

"I know. Talk to you later, Marilyn."

"That you will."

After I ended the call, I crossed to the windows at the side of the house. I looked out at the thick falling snow piling up on the balsam trees along the edge of the lawn. Tom Daniels was the very man who headed up the investment company that was under federal investigation.

Much to my chagrin, I'd stumbled across information that wasn't going to play well for him. While I didn't work directly for Tom, my investment company was part of an umbrella consortium with his. So, I was officially a whistleblower. What I didn't know was how many other companies were implicated. The only thing I knew was mine wasn't. I had already volunteered to turn over any funds earned through the consortium investments tied to the fraud. It was not fun to be a whistleblower, but I hated cheats.

Some people assumed that because my father was in jail for fraud, I was perfectly comfortable with it myself. They didn't realize what happened with my father had only sharpened my distaste for it. Shaking my head, I turned and walked down the hallway to the kitchen.

The minute I stepped through the archway into the room, my gaze was drawn like a lodestone to Jane. She was sitting at the table by the windows. Her hair was twisted into a bun, and she'd stuck a pen through it. Loose tendrils hung around her neck and cheeks, and her glasses were on. She looked all very studious and proper, and I wanted to fuck her.

In fact, I wanted to stand her up and bend her over the kitchen table. Maybe not the first time. Perhaps the second, third, fourth, or fifth. This need for Jane was not going to be chased out of my system by mental willpower; that much I was discovering.

She looked over, pressing her finger against her glasses, and I decided she needed to keep her glasses on when I fucked her. They were a massive turn-on. They were perfect; she was perfect. We stared at each other, and it felt as if a charge was lit in the air. I took a breath and dipped my chin in acknowledgment.

"Getting some lunch," I commented.

"Okay. I heated up some lasagna."

I looked at the clock and realized it was two in the afternoon. "You did?" I turned to look at her again.

She nodded. "It's in the oven right now. I made

some more sauce. It just seemed like a lasagna kind of day."

"It is," I said slowly.

The lasagna with extra sauce was delicious. I didn't need to learn Jane was a really good cook in addition to being sexy as hell and distracting me from all semblance of sanity. After lunch, I returned to work on cutting the trim. The house had over thirty rooms, so there was plenty to do. Unfortunately, I was preoccupied.

Between my phone call earlier from work, the snow falling, and the house feeling oddly small, I couldn't stop thinking about Jane. My thoughts felt like a game of ping pong. I would hit the ball away from Jane, or rather my attraction to her, and it would bounce it right back. It didn't matter how many times I hit the ball because it always bounced back as if attached by a string. Hell, I felt like *she* had an invisible string attached to me. I was at the other end of the house, far enough away that I couldn't even hear if she left the kitchen or walked upstairs. Yet I felt her presence the entire time.

My resolve was weakening, and I was starting to see her point. She wasn't asking for anything amazing nor did she have any expectations. And I got it. I absolutely did. This would be a barrier to her dating unless she wanted to satisfy someone's fetish for a virgin.

You're fucking insane, my sarcastic angel chimed in. *You're just looking for an excuse to fuck her.*

Maybe so, but what's wrong with that? She actually asked me to, my naughty angel said.

My good angel remained quiet after that in the corner of my mind. I didn't precisely understand my own reservations at Jane's request anymore. Aside from this burning-hot yearning for Jane, I liked her. I really did. I could imagine something else with her.

Once that idea was formed, it hung there in my thoughts, a possibility that I both craved and repelled. It was early evening when I finally decided to quit. I had been working all day and had the trim cut for most of the windows downstairs. It was stacked in orderly rows against the wall. I turned off my tools and dusted my hands on my jeans, peering out the window.

The snow was still falling. We had to have at least a foot and a half now. I slid my phone out of my pocket and quickly texted our plow guy to ask him to wait until this was completely over. We didn't need to go anywhere, and there was no sense in wasting money on an extra plow. The driveway was long enough as it was.

I heard footsteps in the hallway, and it felt as if a thousand tiny flames flickered to life inside my body. Air rushed in as the flames gathered force.

Jane stopped in the doorway. Curling one hand around the doorframe, she peered into the room. "Oh, you have this set up as a workspace," she commented

"Yep." I was standing by the windows and swung one arm in an arc toward the windows. "See, these all need to be replaced. They've been painted over too many times. Some of the windowsills are rotten."

"That's quite the project." Her hand dropped from the doorframe, and she lifted her knuckles, pressing them to her glasses. She walked into the room. "Are you doing all of this by yourself?"

I shrugged. "We've all done a little bit of work here and there, but I volunteered to handle the windows. Considering my work schedule, it'll probably take me a year or two to get them all done, but that's okay. There's no need to rush."

Jane stopped a few feet away, sliding her hands in

the back pockets of her jeans. That action had the effect of pulling her shoulder blades back and pushing her breasts forward. She was wearing this fluffy, soft sweater with a V-neck. I wanted to cross over to her and slide my hands under it, knowing I would find her silky, warm skin underneath.

"It's still snowing," she commented.

She took another few steps, stopping beside me and looking out the windows. She wasn't teasing or flirting, not even a little. But the effect she had on me by coming closer was like pouring gas on a fire, sending the flames flickering higher and higher.

"How's your day been?" I heard myself asking, my voice coming out gruff

She lifted a shoulder in an elegant shrug as she angled to face me, her lips curling in a slight smile and sending a sizzle of heat through me. I forced my mind to stay on track. Not that it was all that important, but I needed something to keep me from plastering her to the wall and kissing her senseless.

"What were you working on?" I managed.

"Getting the syllabi ready and loading things into the university's online system. It's similar to the one I used before, but it helps me to get familiar with it."

I nodded politely, still attempting to keep my attention focused on the conversation, but I was distracted as her scent drifted to me. It was a subtle floral scent, mingling with an underlying musky hint. My eyes dropped to the side of her neck. My mouth almost watered because I wanted to kiss her, to taste that sweet skin.

"Ian?" Jane prompted.

I dragged my eyes to hers. "What?"

"You didn't say anything else."

I should've been embarrassed or, at the least,

disconcerted by her catching me in such complete distraction. I had no clue how long I'd been simply standing there staring at her. Because I was foolish, or stupid, or both, I stepped closer to her, lifting a hand and dragging my knuckles lightly along her collarbone.

A pink flush bloomed on her cheeks, and I heard the little puff of air that escaped her lips. Her eyes flicked to mine, darkening. "What are you doing?"

I didn't know what I was doing, or maybe I did. I let my palm uncurl, tracing along the collar of her sweater and down to the bottom of the V. My finger-tips feathered underneath the soft fabric along the curve of her breast. "Touching you," I murmured.

She cleared her throat. "Is that a good idea?" she whispered.

I shrugged. "Maybe not, but maybe so. I've been thinking."

"About what?" Her voice was a ragged whisper, and I could see the rapid beat of her pulse at the base of her throat.

I couldn't resist dipping my head and dusting a kiss there, and then letting my lips trail over to her collarbone. Because her skin was sweet, and she made this inarticulate sound in her throat when she arched toward me.

"I've reconsidered your proposition."

Jane stilled, but she didn't move away, and I let my hand slide into her sweater, at which point I almost growled when I discovered she wasn't even wearing a bra. Her skin was silky soft, her nipple already puck-ering into my touch when I cupped her breast lightly. I couldn't resist letting my thumb barely graze over that taut little peak.

"I think maybe it's a good idea," I said against her throat, savoring the way she shivered. I forced myself to lift my hand. "We should have some ground rules, though."

She blinked at me before nodding quickly. "Okay, I'll start."

Oh, my fucking God. This woman was a virgin, for crying out loud. She was so prim and bossy. Of course, she would want to start with the rules.

"Perfect, tell me your rules," I replied.

"Only here in Haven's Bay. Just once, but if we like it—" She paused, clearing her throat. "Well, we have a few weeks together. You can't tell anyone. Not Thea, not your brothers, not anyone."

It took more effort than I wanted to admit not to shove her sweater down and suck her sweet nipple into my mouth. I tightened my grip on the reins of my control and nodded. "Agreed. I have a rule too. Wear your glasses."

Her brow furrowed, her eyes questioning. "What?"

"I like them. That's my ground rule."

"But what if they get in the way?" she asked, biting her lip.

"You're fucking sexy as hell with them. If I decide to take them off, I will."

I could practically see tiny wheels spinning in her brain as she considered this. "Only *you* can take them off?" she countered.

I couldn't resist tasting her again and dipped my head to lightly nip her neck. She shivered and arched into me. My lips curled in a smile when I lifted my head. "Yes. Only me."

She rolled her eyes. "Fine. But I think it's a little bossy."

"You haven't even seen bossy yet," I teased.

I finally, fucking *finally*, kissed her again. This was just a kiss, a little kindling on the fire. Yet there was no *little* about anything between us. The second her tongue teased against mine, I was pulling her fast against me. She was warm and soft, and we devoured each other. I had no idea how long we stood there kissing.

By the time awareness punctured the need blazing like a fire in my brain, I'd tugged her sweater down, and both of her breasts were plumped over it. Her nipples were pink and damp, and I'd unzipped her pants and dipped my fingers into her core to find her slick with arousal.

I wanted to fuck her right here, right now—to bend her over my worktable and take her roughly. But she was a virgin, and I didn't want to be rough about any of it. I shackled my rampaging need and drew my fingers out.

I couldn't help it. I had to taste her, so I lifted my hand and drew my fingers into my mouth, letting out a satisfied hum at her tangy and salty taste. Her eyes widened as she stared at me, her breath coming in ragged gasps.

Chapter Twelve

JANE

My heart was pounding so fast, every beat tumbled into the next. I could hardly get a breath in. Little bonfires lit on the surface of my skin, and I was already on fire, the flames licking higher and higher inside.

When Ian lifted his hand and licked my arousal off his fingers, my knees went weak, and my pussy clenched. I didn't even know if I could make it through this encounter with him.

His gaze swept over me as he lowered his hands slowly. I adjusted my sweater, tugging it up. My breasts bounced below the collar again.

His eyes darkened, and his mouth twisted slightly. "Pity. That's okay. I'm going to see all of you soon."

Then he was reaching for my hand, and our footsteps echoed as we walked down the hallway. He led me up the stairs into the master bedroom. He closed the door behind us, the sound of the latch clicking loudly in the room.

Throughout this home, all of the ceilings were tall. With the hardwood floors and sparse furnishings, any sound echoed easily. Although I'd been so swept into the rushing current of desire that I'd forgotten myself just moments ago, my self-consciousness came crashing back.

My hands curled into small fists, and I squeezed them together before stretching them open. Maybe I hadn't gotten to the full act, but I'd had plenty of experience with foreplay. I already knew that no one I'd been with even came close to the fiery inferno of need that burned between Ian and me. He kicked off his shoes before turning to look at me. I was wearing a pair of slippers and stepped out of them. We stared at each other from where we were standing at the foot of the bed.

It felt as if we were all alone in this room, in this world, with the snow swirling outside and the sound of the wind coming in rhythmic gusts off the ocean. It was winter, and we were alone on this windswept coast.

Without a word, Ian crossed over to the fireplace. I watched as he efficiently built a fire using the wood stacked in a small rack by the wall. When he straightened and turned to me, his lips kicked up at a corner, promptly sending my belly into a spinning somersault.

"There. Now it'll be even warmer."

He hooked his hand behind his head, catching the back of his shirt and yanking it up over his head. My mouth went dry as I stared at him shirtless. He was muscled and lean, his skin bronzed with a dusting of dark hair across the muscled planes of his chest and then arrowing down to disappear behind the waistband of his jeans. His arousal was evident, and I clenched again, feeling slick arousal at my core. My pulse galloped along, and I took in a shallow breath of air when I lifted my eyes to his.

I moved to curl my hands around the bottom of my sweater, but he shook his head.

"Wait."

He crossed over to me, lifting his hand and pulling out the pen that I'd stuck in my hair somewhere along the way. It fell to the floor with a clatter as my hair tumbled loose. On the heels of hardly a breath, his hands were sliding through my loose locks, and his mouth was on mine again.

I forgot everything outside of this very moment. His lips on mine. The bold sweep of his tongue gliding against mine. His hard body coming close, and the heat and power of him a potent, shimmering force around me.

His hand slid free of my hair, moving down my back in a smooth pass. He cupped my bottom, giving it a firm squeeze when he rocked his arousal into the cradle of my hips. I let out something between a moan and a gasp into our kiss. He lifted his head, and in another moment, he was stepping away. I felt almost bereft.

His hands slid down along my sides, curling over the waistband of my jeans. His motions were swift and efficient as he unbuttoned them. They were off in a flash, and I was stepping free. His hands reversed direction, moving up. My belly trembled under his touch as he pushed my sweater up, lifting it in a smooth motion. It sailed in an arc through the air before falling to the floor in a rumple.

I was naked except for my panties and socks, and Ian was kissing me again. I forgot to be self-conscious. I felt my knees bump against the back of the bed.

He was driving me absolutely wild, teasing me with his lips and teeth and tongue behind my ear, sending shivers chasing throughout my body and little bonfires lighting over the surface of my skin. I was hot and cold and needy, aroused to the point of feeling frantic. My breasts pressed against his chest when I took a deep breath. I was so overcome with the sensations that I was almost frozen in it, caught as if in the eye of a storm while nothing but turmoil and chaos surrounded me.

Habit broke through when I lifted my hand to push my glasses up my nose. His eyes were dark before he leaned down and nipped lightly on the side of my neck. He stepped back swiftly and shoved his jeans down. My eyes dropped to see his arousal, blatantly visible through his fitted briefs.

For several echoing beats of my heart, time felt suspended in a fiery, shimmering curtain. We stared at each other. Air was in short supply, and I took a shuddering breath. Goose bumps were rising on my skin, yet I was *sooo* hot. It felt as if I'd been blasted by a wall of fire.

Ian stepped closer as my hand fell from pushing up my glasses. His gaze made a quick sweep down my body, and my toes curled when his eyes made their way back to mine. My nipples tightened, and I felt achy and restless all over. He took another step closer and lifted his hand.

"Can I take these off?" He lightly tapped the side of my glasses with his forefinger.

I narrowed my eyes. "I thought you said you wanted them on." I felt a little saucy as I stared at him.

His lips curled in a slow grin sending the butterflies in my belly into a mad spin. "I said I wanted to be the one who decided if you took them off," he clarified. "I do love them."

"You like the nerdy girl look?" I offered.

He shook his head quickly. "No, darlin'. I like *you*."

Then his lips were teasing along the side of my neck, and I was whimpering when he carefully removed my glasses. He stepped away to place them on the dresser.

Just as I heard the clink of them on the wooden surface, he glanced back at me. "You can see, right?" he asked.

With the combination of raw desire and anxiety about what was happening pushing at every corner inside, I found that hysterical. It took the edge off my nerves when I burst out laughing as I nodded. "Yes," I managed when I stopped laughing. "I read a lot, and they help with reading. It's not like I can't see without them."

He turned and walked back toward me, and I soaked him in. Jesus. Desire swept through me swiftly, like the tide rushing in. He was so sexy. With his arms swinging as he walked, my eyes lingered on his muscled shoulders before trailing down over the planes of his chest. I swallowed as my gaze dipped lower and greedily soaked in his thick arousal outlined by his briefs.

It was *much*; he was *so* much. Uncertainty started to slide into my awareness, and I wondered if I'd been crazy to propose this.

As if he could read my mind, Ian shook his head. "I don't know what you're thinking but stop right now."

Chapter Thirteen

IAN

Jane took a quick breath, letting it out in a shuddery gust. Her gorgeous eyes blinked at me with her lips curling in just the barest hint of a smile. Even though I promised myself I wasn't going to rush this, I still needed to touch her. Right this very second.

I let my hand slide through her silky gold hair, over the curve of her shoulder and down her side, teasing over the swell of her breast and the dip of her waist. Feeling greedy, I cupped her bottom, giving it a little squeeze when I rocked my aching arousal into her.

She let out a needy little sigh, and I set out to make her feel everything, to make this so good she wouldn't forget. Feathering along the edges of my thoughts was a hint of danger. I needed to be careful, not just for Jane but also for myself. Because this was *so* good. This chemistry was like a shooting flare in the sky, one that never burned out. Every touch kindled the fire hotter and hotter, and all I wanted was more, more, and *more*.

I took deep pulls from her mouth, savoring how she threw herself into our kisses. Her tongue was a sensual tease as I nibbled on her bottom lip. I reluc-tantly drew away from her mouth and teased along the sensitive skin of her neck. I loved it when she arched into me and whimpered. She wasn't the kind of woman who let go easily. That was already evident.

We were still standing at the foot of the bed when I cupped her breasts and lowered my head to lave at one nipple and then the other, teasing and playing with them until she was arching and crying out. My thoughts were barely coherent, but I had enough sense to stretch her out on the bed when my own knees almost buckled.

I mapped Jane's body with my lips and my palms, finding every curve and learning every sensitive spot. Her belly trembled under my touch when I slid my hand down, dipping into her cotton panties to find her dripping with arousal, soaked for me. There was no point in kidding myself that keeping her panties on would keep me sane, so I dragged them down her legs, and she helpfully kicked them free. Then I made my way back up, dropping hot kisses on her calves, teasing the sensitive skin just inside her knee and on the insides of her thighs.

Her pussy was pink, wet, and quivering. I pushed one knee to the side and trailed my fingers through her swollen folds before bringing my mouth to her, gratified at her sharp, keening cry when I sank two fingers into her, knuckle deep. She was restless under my touch, her head thrashing and her hips trembling. She came faster than I expected, her entire body going taut before she cried out my name and rippled around my fingers as she shuddered all over.

I stayed with her until the trembling stopped, then slowly drew my fingers away. The taste and scent of her consumed my senses. As soon as I moved, rising on to an elbow, her eyes fluttered open, and her heavy-lidded gaze met mine. She was quiet, just watching me. I straightened and finally ditched my boxers, tossing them on the floor.

By some miracle, I'd thought ahead and had condoms. I snagged a condom out of the top drawer of the dresser, rolling it on swiftly. By the time I turned back toward the bed, I could tell Jane had started thinking.

I shifted my hips onto the bed, swinging my legs up and leaning back on the pillows. She shimmied closer, curling onto her knees. "What?" she asked.

"You're thinking too much," I teased lightly.

She was already flushed all over, but the pink deepened, and she lifted a shoulder in a bashful shrug. "Maybe we should stop right now," I said, entirely serious.

She shook her head quickly. "Don't you dare."

Angling toward her, I brushed her tangled hair away from her eyes, tucking a few loose locks behind her ear. I decided to make her forget the details again. Dipping my head, I teased my lips and tongue along her collarbone. I cupped a breast, savoring the lush weight and letting my palm graze over the nipple. I just barely nipped right behind her ear. I'd already discovered she loved that.

She responded instantly, letting out a ragged whimper and arching toward me. I tugged her onto my lap, and she shifted until she was straddling me. I didn't rush. I played with her breasts again, teasing her nipples to damp peaks until she was rocking her hips restlessly over my arousal. It was hard to admit, but my control was nearing its end. The frayed thread was about to snap, but I clung to it because I wasn't going to ruin this. I let my hands slide down from her delectable breasts, finally gripping her hips slightly and asking in a gruff whisper, "Are you sure about this?"

"Yes!" she demanded, her eyes flying open.

She gave me a bossy look, and it was like a whip cracking behind me. I wanted to let the reins snap loose, but I held tight to what little control I had. She rose up, and I nudged into her slick entrance. I knew she was as ready as she could be. She was wet, so wet, but still, I waited.

She let out a restless hum as she shifted her hips down over me. I had to grit my teeth not to thrust upward and fill her instantly. She was tight, so very tight. Another moment later, she let out a frustrated gasp. She moved swiftly, driving her hips down and letting out a startled gasp. I watched her when she stiffened slightly. But she held still, biting her lip as her eyes fell closed.

The need to take over, to claim this moment was pushing at me. I swallowed, thinking through the storm of sensation sizzling in every cell. "You okay?" I managed.

She nodded, just barely. She breathed in deeply once and then again. I felt her channel relax in increments around me.

Fuck me. This was beyond good. Her silky tight heat clenched around me. She wiggled her hips, seating herself more deeply. I was buried to the hilt, and I still hadn't moved. Her eyes met mine through thick, honey lashes.

"Wow. There." Her voice was breathy, but she sounded satisfied.

I couldn't help my lips when they kicked up into a smile. "*There* is one way to put it."

She bit her lip and laughed a little. My hands were still on her hips, my fingertips pressing into the soft give of her curves. She held still for another few beats and then started to move. Finally, fucking finally, I gripped her hips and nudged into her, the subtle motion nearly pushing me over the edge instantly. We began rocking together. I nudged into her deeply, again and again and again. Her breasts were pressed against me with every shift.

I watched the surprise flit across her face just before she bit her lip and started to tremble. Her channel tightened around me. She was so wet, her swollen clit was sliding against me with every tiny motion we made. I released one hand and teased my fingers in a swirl right where we were joined. My balls were drawn up tight, and my release was threatening as electricity sizzled at the base of my spine.

She moaned, and then her eyes flew wide with a surprised cry. She shuddered over me, her pussy clamping around my cock. I finally let go, my release hitting me like a lightning strike, hard and fast. I curled my arm around her, burying my head in her neck while I shuddered roughly. The release was more intense than any I'd ever experienced because I'd been holding on for so long.

She rested against me, a warm bundle in my arms, and I absorbed the tremors running through her body. I pressed kisses along the base of her neck and breathed her in. When I felt her lift her head, I followed, leaning back against the headboard. Her gaze met mine, a little surprised, a little hazed. Her lips curled into a slow smile.

"There," she repeated.

"There?" Ian returned, a lilt of a question in his voice.

I felt replete and sated. The pleasure of that encounter was indescribable. My nerve endings felt oversensitive, almost as if I couldn't take it if anything else happened because it was too good. I'd known from the very first kiss that the chemistry between us was powerful.

But chemistry didn't mean much sometimes. That was a part of why I was still a virgin or, rather, had been until just now. Because some kisses told me right away that it wasn't worth it. With Ian, every single second was incredible.

His fingers sifted through the ends of my hair. The gesture, though idle, felt intimate. I did a mental inventory of my body. I felt so relaxed, so easy. I thought I should feel tense, almost businesslike in the aftermath.

My very comfort sent threads of tension through me. As if he could read my mind, Ian said, "You're thinking."

I rolled my head to the side, catching his eyes. "Of course, I'm thinking. Aren't you thinking?"

His lips kicked up at one corner, and dammit if butterflies didn't spin in my belly. "Not thinking too much. Sometimes it's good just to relax, you know."

I swallowed and nodded. Even though a tiny bell was clanging a warning, all I wanted to do was curl up with him and forget the rest of the world.

———

My feet were tucked under my knees on the couch, and I held a glass of wine in my hand as I sipped it. We'd had a busy afternoon between Ian going with me to finally take a good look at my parents' house and picking up my car from Joe's garage late this afternoon. To my relief, the house had mostly been buttoned down. Ian had helped me move the few boxes left behind by my parents into a storage area in the basement here, and I'd called my parents with an update. Now, it was dark outside, and we were relaxing and watching basketball.

"Yes!" he exclaimed, punching a fist into the air.

I chuckled, and his eyes slid sideways to mine. "What?"

"Nothing. I didn't know you were a basketball fan."

He shrugged, almost sheepishly, as he leaned back into the couch cushions. "I like it. It's distracting, plus it's something completely not part of my life."

"What do you mean?"

"My life is busy, filled with numbers and stress and counting and worrying about things like that. Watching a sport is entirely removed from my life."

"Do you like all sports?"

He shrugged. "I'll watch anything, but I like the pace of basketball the most."

I sipped my wine. "I can't recall. Did you play sports in high school?"

"I ran track. I wasn't that great. I didn't have enough discipline. Total middle of the pack guy as far as my speed. What about you?"

I lowered my wine glass. "What about me?" I prompted.

"Did you play any sports in high school?"

His brows hitched up when I shook my head. "None at all?" he pressed.

I rolled my eyes. "No, and this is why you didn't even recognize me at first."

He looked affronted. "That's not fair. I graduated from high school fourteen years ago." I opened my mouth to argue some random point, but he shook his head. He reached over, curling his arm over my shoulder and sliding his fingers into my hair. "Don't give me hell for not recognizing you. I would have. It's just I didn't expect to see you here in my family's home over the holidays."

Heat flared in my cheeks when his thumb teased along the side of my neck right behind my ear. It sent a hot shiver through me. "Okay," I managed to reply, hoping it wasn't too breathy.

"Plus, you were a freshman when I was a senior."

"Right, that's decades," I countered dryly.

Ian rolled his eyes, his intent gaze on me. There was something about being encompassed in his attention. He was thorough, very thorough, and I knew that intimately now. I also sensed I'd underestimated him. He was a perceptive man, and I suddenly felt skittish under his gaze as if he could read more into me than I could read into him.

"I was focused on my grades in high school, not sports. I probably should've done some sports," I said finally.

"What would you have done?"

"I have no idea. Maybe swimming. I've always loved swimming."

His eyes shifted to look out the back window into the darkness. It had started to snow. Again. "No swimming right now," he commented.

I laughed. "No, definitely not. It's freezing out."

"We'll have to come back in the summer."

"We?"

Chapter Fifteen

IAN

I shifted my attention back to Jane, away from the darkness with the snow illuminated by the lights out the window. I hadn't been thinking when I said we should come back in the summer.

My heart twisted in my chest as I looked over at this girl beside me. She was a woman now, no longer the girl I didn't pay much attention to in high school.

It was true that I had made a point of not paying attention to any of Thea's friends. We'd been at odds for most of our childhood, the two youngest in the family and frequently clashing. We were close now, and our relationship was different, but I didn't know any of her current friends. I didn't like thinking that I probably wouldn't have noticed Jane, even if she hadn't been Thea's friend.

Now, I couldn't stop thinking about her at all. I recalled more details about her from high school—always wearing glasses, always quiet. She even worked part-time in the library at the school.

"Yes, we," I finally answered.

"Us being here at the same time now was just a chance," Jane replied.

"I call it serendipitous," I offered, not sure why I was pressing this. It chafed at me that she was trying to compartmentalize me.

"Oh, how?"

I hadn't been planning any of this with Jane. But here we were now, and I'd just had the best night I'd had since I could remember. Tonight brought back memories of when I was younger, but not because I had amazing sexual experiences. Most guys didn't. We were all fumbling and probably careless, but I recalled the hum of anticipation, the kind of excitement that came from something new that you couldn't replicate.

This night with Jane was filled with new moments, though perhaps not new for me in the way it was for her. I still kind of couldn't believe she was a virgin and was no more. I'd fallen into a pattern when it came to sex, treating it solely as a way to meet needs, the way someone might grab dinner or take a quick shower when they were in a hurry.

I'd savored every second of tonight. I'd forgotten what that was like. I didn't want this to be compartmentalized to only tonight.

Jane's eyes dropped from mine. She lifted her wine glass and took a swallow. I couldn't seem to take my hand away once I had touched her. Her skin was soft and silky along the side of her neck.

The fire in the fireplace cast a flickering glow over us. The basketball game carried on, with the sounds of cheering and the announcers following the game receding into the background.

When her lashes lifted and her eyes met mine again, my heart gave a swift kick. She had her glasses back on, and I wished I could climb inside her mind and read her thoughts. She was good at keeping her thoughts shuttered away.

"I still don't get it," I heard myself saying.

Her brows hitched. "Get what?"

"Okay, I *do* understand what you said before, that some guys would get skittish about someone reading too much into being someone's first. But I'm surprised nobody has locked you down yet."

She pressed her lips together, laughing softly as she rolled her eyes. "Locked me down?"

"Yeah. You're gorgeous, you're smart, you have a good career, you're financially stable, and you're fucking hot."

Pink crested high on her cheeks as she stared at me. Her gaze flicked away, and she glanced at her wine glass before finishing the last swallow. When she leaned over to set it on the coffee table, my hand fell away from her neck. I wasn't to be deterred. As soon as she straightened, I shifted closer to her, pulling her toward me at the same time.

"What are you doing?" she murmured, looking flustered.

"I like being close to you," I said bluntly.

"This was just a one-time thing," she countered.

"Did we say it was a one-time thing?"

She bit her lip, sending a sizzle of fire through my veins. "I thought we had ground rules."

"I didn't think we said it was only once."

She twisted her lips when she nodded. I was being reckless, but I ignored it. It's just this was too good with Jane, and I wanted more. We hadn't said only once, and I knew she knew that. Feathering along the edges of my thoughts was a subtle warning, pointing out this wasn't just about how good this felt. I was in no mood to entertain warnings.

"Nobody's here. It's snowing. We might as well enjoy the time."

As Jane stared up at me, her lips parted. I didn't wait, dipping my head and catching her little gasp when I fit my mouth over hers. Our kiss spiraled out of control almost instantly. Before I knew it, I had pulled her onto my lap to straddle me, and my arousal swelled to an ache.

One kiss melted into another and then another. I refrained from burying myself inside her again after we'd tugged our clothes out of the way. I knew she could be sensitive, so I tasted the core of her until she came in a shuddering burst. She thoroughly disabused me of any notion that she hadn't had experience other than the full act after she left me nearly incoherent with her hands and mouth on my cock.

We fell asleep together. That was the first of every night together over the following weeks.

Jane peered up at me, pressing her glasses up on her nose. "Ian, I don't know." Her lashes swept down, and her toe tapped nervously on the floor.

"You don't know what?" I prompted as I reached for her hands.

"It just feels weird."

"You're going to spend Christmas with us. Thea will love it," I pressed.

"Yeah, but then she's going to wonder." Jane circled her hand in the air and looked back up at me.

"Wonder what?"

"If we're together." The flush that rose swiftly on her cheeks set my heart to thumping hard.

"That's fine with me. Let's just have this conversation right now. This"—I gestured back and forth between us—"is not ending just because you're going to start your new job in Boston and I'm going back to DC."

"That's against the ground rules," she said, her lips curling into a saucy smile.

I shrugged. "I don't care. We made those ground rules before we knew things were going to change."

Her gaze was skeptical, and she let out a soft breath. "Ian, you have a whole life in DC."

"I don't have to stay there."

I hadn't talked to Jane about a lot of things. In particular, one giant issue—the stupid whistleblower investigation I was caught in the middle of. I wanted to tell her, but I literally couldn't, or I would get in legal trouble. The knowledge of that secret felt like a sharp splinter caught under a nail.

Ignoring that worry—because I truly could do nothing about it for now—I stepped closer, releasing one of her hands and nudging my knuckles under her chin. "Look at me," I murmured while my heart banged against my ribs.

I hadn't even thought through what I wanted to say. It still bothered me that I hadn't recognized her instantly that first night here at the house. Because, now, I'd never forget her, and I knew if I let her slip away, I'd regret it for the rest of my life.

Maybe I hadn't planned this, and maybe I hadn't known the chemistry that had started a bonfire between us was about so much more. Everything with Jane felt right, and I didn't want it to end. I wasn't sure how we would make it work, but I was determined we *were* going to make it work.

"You know what I mean," I whispered when she lifted her eyes up to mine. Her gaze softened. My lips were moving against hers when I spoke again. "I'm falling for you. I don't think I'm alone."

I forced myself to stay quiet and wait, although impatience was clawing at me.

"You're not," she finally whispered back.

Chapter Seventeen

JANE

"Okay, that'll be all for today. Any questions before we finish up?"

I scanned the classroom before glancing down at my laptop. The university had a combination of live classes with some students being remote. Those online could raise their hand on the screen. A number of thumbs-up appeared on the screen, but no questions, so I glanced back at the classroom. "All right, so we'll meet next week. Same time, same place, same bat-channel."

The students filed out, and I returned to my office to finish checking in on a few things. My phone vibrated on my desk. Spinning it around, I automatically curled my lips into a smile when I saw Ian's text on the screen.

Ian: *I'll be there.*

A subtle anticipation began to hum through my body. I still couldn't believe we were doing this. But so far, it was actually working. We alternated taking the train every other weekend to see each other. I loved taking the train. For one, it allowed us both to work on the trip, and it was much faster than driving.

I didn't know where it was going to lead with us, but it felt good. Thea teased me all the time. We were actually meeting her for dinner tonight, so I was prepared for more teasing. I tapped out my reply.

Me: *Good. Can't wait to see you.*

I rushed through a few last-minute emails before closing my laptop. Both of us would do a little work over the weekend. That was another thing that worked with us. We both had busy jobs and sometimes had to check in on the weekends. I walked home, a huge plus with this job. I'd always loved Boston as a city, but I was finding I really loved living here. From the outside, it seemed like it would be hard to live here, but it was a great city with a large selection of restaurants and other activities within walking distance.

My apartment occupied the upper floor in a down-town brownstone, and I loved it. It had beautiful hard-wood floors and windows tall enough to stand inside. It had been upgraded with modern appliances although it still had the old fireplace with a gorgeous granite mantel.

I called Thea while I was waiting for Ian to arrive. "So, where do you want to meet?" I asked after we checked in with each other.

"I haven't had a good steak in a while," she replied.

"Ooh, perfect. You know I love steak."

"Are you sure you want to have dinner with me the first night Ian gets here?" Thea prompted.

"Of course! I haven't seen you in weeks, and I see him every weekend."

She laughed softly. "I know. You two are getting serious."

I was relieved she couldn't see my face because I felt the heat rush into my cheeks. It felt like we *were* getting serious, and I wasn't sure what I thought about that. I liked Ian—a lot.

In fact, I was pretty sure I was falling for him, big time.

On the list of things I hadn't planned for, falling for Ian was probably at the top. Oh sure, I thought I wanted to be serious with someone someday. I even thought I wanted to have kids. It's just a serious relationship had seemed to be a far-off, distant possibility. And now, I was falling for one of my childhood friend's older brothers, a guy I'd never even considered.

"I know. I'm not sure what I think about it," I replied honestly. "Don't you dare tease me about it in front of him."

I could practically feel my friend rolling her eyes through the phone line. "Fine. Back to dinner. I can't remember the name of it, but there's a good place just down the street from where you live."

"We should meet in an hour," I replied.

"Sounds like a plan. I'll call ahead to make a reservation. See you soon."

Only minutes after Thea hung up the phone, I heard a light knock on the door followed by the sound of a key sliding in. Ian had a key to my apartment, and he'd gotten me a key to his. We'd made that call when he had a late meeting one night when I was visiting him.

"Jane," he called as soon as I heard the door opening.

Because I was *that* excited to see him, I rushed out of the bathroom, practically skidding to a stop in front of him.

"Hey," I said breathlessly.

His lips curled in a smile as he stepped closer and folded me into his arms. He smelled good. He carried the scent of the fresh spring air with him. The train station was a few blocks away.

"You must've walked fast," I murmured into his chest before leaning my head back.

He shrugged. "I sort of jogged."

I eyed him. "You did?"

He shrugged. "Yeah, I wanted to see you." He lifted me into his arms as he spun me around and slipped my hips on to a wide half-wall that served as a divider between the entryway and the living room. "I'm always in a hurry to see you."

I opened my mouth to reply, and then he was kissing me. I completely forgot myself for a minute. By the time he pulled away, I was hot all over and restless. I took in a gulping breath and shook my head to clear the haze.

"We're meeting Thea in a half hour for dinner."

"That soon?" He looked downright disappointed.

"You're the one who said you wanted to have dinner with her," I pointed out.

Chapter Eighteen

IAN

I stared into Jane's eyes, willing my need for her to abate. I had suggested dinner with my sister because I hadn't seen her in a month now. I felt a little conflicted about it because I was seeing Jane every weekend. But right here, right now, I just wanted Jane all to myself.

Jane's lips curled in a sly smile. "You can handle it. We can't cancel. I just talked to her, and we're getting steak."

I let my forehead fall into the sweet curve of her neck and took a deep breath, inhaling her scent. Lifting my head, I pressed a quick kiss to her lips. Because if I let that kiss linger, my discipline, shaky as it already was, might fail me.

"Steak sounds delicious. Let's go," I said firmly.

Forcing myself to step back, I turned and lifted the bag I'd dropped on the floor when I came in. "I'll just put this away."

She nodded as she smoothed a hand over her hair. I walked down the short hallway off the living room area and dropped my bag in her bedroom. Occasionally, I experienced twinges of doubt. Not because I had any doubts about how I felt about Jane and how things were going with us, but because it was so unexpected. If anyone had told me I'd hand over the key to my apartment to a woman before I'd gone to that much-needed holiday break in Haven's Bay a few months ago, I'd have told them they were fucking out of their mind.

Yet when I had to work late one night and knew Jane's train was arriving, she ended up having to wait for half an hour before I could get there. The next morning, I'd gone to a hardware store and gotten a copy made for her before she even woke up. Giving up a weekend with her was out of the question. When I returned to the living room, she was sliding into a lightweight jacket and stepping into her boots.

"You shouldn't have worn jeans," I commented as I approached her, appreciating the way her hips filled out the denim.

She turned, cocking her head to the side. "What do you mean?"

"They're harder to take off, especially with boots on."

Pink tinged her cheeks, and she rolled her eyes. "Well, I'm not changing now."

I shrugged. "Just saying. I'm all about easy access with you."

She gave me a saucy grin. "It's a good thing I'm wearing jeans because you need to keep your hands to yourself at dinner with Thea."

I grinned and copped a quick feel of her sweet bottom. She rolled her eyes again and bit her lip, which meant I *had* to kiss her before we walked out of her apartment.

"I don't know about the dinner and jeans. Skirts

are a better option. You know what I mean," I said once we were walking hand in hand on the sidewalk.

"Ian!" she exclaimed.

I chuckled and squeezed her hand. I loved teasing her. The last time we'd had dinner with one of my siblings, it had been Dallas, and she'd been wearing a skirt. I might've gotten a little handsy under the table.

"Did you wear jeans on purpose?" That thought belatedly occurred to me.

Jane let out a sly laugh before shaking her head. "I wish I could say I thought about that, but it's Friday and they're comfortable."

The conversation shifted into the mundane of catching up. We texted and usually talked almost every day. But I loved seeing her at the end of the week and catching up on the details of life. It was bothering me that I couldn't tell her what was going on at work. I didn't like holding anything back from her, and it felt like a tiny splinter in my awareness. There was still plenty to talk about.

"You're liking it here in Boston then?" I asked as we rounded a corner onto the street that would lead us to the restaurant where we were meeting Thea.

She glanced up at me. "I am. It's a good fit. Plus, I have friends here. It's been really nice to reconnect with Thea, Sasha, and Audrey."

Although things felt really good with her, the awareness that we might need to make a decision about where we lived occasionally hung in the air between us. If we took things to the next level, one of us might have to make a change. I'd already made up my mind that I would move to Boston because I could, but I wasn't sure Jane was ready to hear that.

"This is it, right?" Jane asked, pausing in front of a newer restaurant in Boston.

I shrugged. "You know better than me."

She tugged me through the doorway. As soon as we stepped inside, we bumped into a crowded area in front of the hostess stand.

"Do you think Thea is already here?" I asked as I glanced at Jane.

Jane nodded. "Yup. She also made reservations."

My stomach growled. "My sister's organizational skills are part of why I love her."

Keeping hold of Jane's hand, I threaded through the cluster in the front, stopping at the hostess stand. "We have reservations under Thea Tate."

The hostess smiled at us. "She's already here. Menus are on the table. Follow me."

We walked behind the hostess through the new space. I glanced around as we made our way across the restaurant, letting out a low whistle. "This is nice. It used to be an old diner, I think."

The hostess glanced over her shoulder, casting me a quick smile. "It did. The renovation transformed it."

"It's beautiful," Jane chimed in.

The server gestured ahead to where Thea was waiting at a booth in the corner. She smiled over at us, waving. As soon as the hostess departed, Thea stood from the table, throwing her arms around me. "Hey, you!" she exclaimed as she stepped back, her blue eyes twinkling.

Thea gave Jane a quick hug, and we sat down across from her in the booth. "You could have brought a date," I commented as I opened the menu.

Thea shrugged nonchalantly. "No date for me."

Jane gave her a curious look but said nothing else. I sensed Thea was holding something back. "You never mention if you're seeing anyone," I added.

"You never talked to me about your dating life

before either. Now, you're with Jane, and I can't get either one of you to say anything about each other," my sister replied tartly.

Jane's cheeks went pink as she looked down at her menu. "We're dating. Isn't that enough for you to know?" I returned.

Thea let out an aggrieved sigh. "I want to know everything."

"Uh, everything?" Jane glanced up quickly.

Thea rolled her eyes. "Okay, maybe not everything, but how is it going?"

"Very well," I said firmly. I slid my arm across Jane's shoulders as I leaned back in the booth. "Now, tell me what's up with life, work, and so on."

My sister shrugged. "I'm busy, and things are okay at work. I'm not loving being at a large law firm. I have a new boss from a different department, and I'm hoping we get along. A good job can turn into a shitty job really fast."

"Don't I know it," Jane offered. "You both heard about my old boss. He wasn't even who hired me, but he was moved over. He was needy and useless all at the same time."

"It seems like you're happy where you are now, though," Thea offered.

Jane nodded. "I am. I have more independence, but things can change."

I simply nodded along. My job had been great until lately. Now, I was seriously considering striking out on my own once the investigation was all over. Fortunately, our conversation moved on to other matters. I didn't have to dwell in my guilt about everything I was withholding about my work.

Every so often, I wondered if Dallas or Noah had caught wind of what was going on. The FBI was involved in the investigation, but it wasn't their office. Even if they knew, they wouldn't be able to ask me about it, and I wouldn't be able to talk to them about it. Not until the team I was dealing with gave me the okay.

I managed to keep my hands mostly to myself during dinner, and Jane only had to swat my hand off her thigh twice. To distract myself, I asked Thea, "So why aren't you seeing anyone?"

Thea leaned back in the booth and took a swallow of her wine while we waited for dinner to arrive. "I didn't say I wasn't."

I cocked my head to the side. "Okay, who?"

"None of your business," she retorted.

"Oh, I'll find out," I countered.

Jane interjected, "We need to plan to have coffee soon."

"You're out of town visiting Ian every other weekend." Thea gestured to me. "Then he's here, and I don't want to do coffee with you and my brother every time I see you. We need girl talk."

Jane laughed softly, glancing over at me. "I've always got work I can do when I'm here on the weekend. I'll just stay at the apartment when you two have coffee," I offered.

"Tomorrow morning then," Jane prompted.

"Deal." Thea lifted her palm to high-five Jane across the table.

A few minutes later, we were eating. "The steaks are chef's kiss," I said. "They even got rare right."

"Well, you don't make it easy. You practically want the cow mooing," my sister offered dryly.

A while after my sister had departed, we were walking home on the sidewalk, and I reached for Jane's hand. Pausing for a moment in front of her, I leaned down to catch her lips in a lingering kiss. When I lifted my head, her cheeks were flushed and her eyes a little hazed.

"What was that for?"

"I just wanted to kiss you. I'm feeling really grateful we ran into each other in Haven's Bay."

"Yeah?"

"Definitely."

Her eyes held mine, and my heart kicked faster. I was getting accustomed to how much I wanted Jane and to the emotion twined within that want, but it still startled me sometimes. After another moment, we turned and continued walking back to her place. Being with her was more comfortable than I had ever expected. I was already impatient to get back to her place so I could have her all to myself.

Chapter Nineteen

JANE

I breathed in the cool spring air with Ian's hand warm around mine as we walked down the street. Darkness had fallen, and the streetlights were on. It felt really nice to have him here.

I was a little skittish sometimes, thinking too much about what was happening for us. I knew I was falling hard and fast for him, and I wasn't sure where he stood or how he felt. Every time work came up, he got tense. I couldn't help but wonder if we got really serious, who would make the move?

I shied away from that train of thought and told myself to just enjoy what we had. Fortunately, that wasn't difficult. The instant he closed the door to my apartment, he spun me around, pressing my back to the door and claiming my mouth in a heated kiss.

I gasped into our kiss. His tongue tangled with mine and his hand slid into my hair, cupping the back of my nape and angling my head to the side. His touch was commanding, with just enough gentleness that it made me want to surrender. Surrendering to Ian was worth every second. Heat was blazing through me when his lips broke free from mine. He gulped in a ragged breath of air, and my head thumped against the door.

A second later, his lips pressed hot, open kisses against the underside of my jaw. His teeth nipped at my earlobe, and he made love to that sensitive spot at the base of my neck as I arched into him. I suddenly regretted my choice of attire. These jeans *were* inconvenient. I was rocking my hips restlessly against him when he curled a palm under my knee and lifted it slightly. The hard ridge of his arousal pressed against my core, sending sharp zings of pleasure through me.

"Ian," I pleaded.

"I told you jeans were a bad idea," he murmured, his chuckle low and sly against the side of my neck.

He tugged at my blouse, undoing my buttons roughly. I felt cool air caressing my breasts when he unclasped my bra. A second later, his mouth closed over a nipple, and I cried out when he gave it a sharp suck.

God! I needed him so much. It seemed like every time we were together, I needed him more. I kept thinking my need would start to lessen, but it only seemed to burn faster and hotter.

He knew me now and how to play my body to its crescendo, just as I knew him. Reaching between us, I managed to undo the buttons on his jeans and slide my hands inside. His shaft was thick with arousal, the skin velvety soft over the hardness. His cock leaped when I curled my hand around it.

"Fuck. Jane," he muttered as he broke free.

He lifted his head. The heat in his eyes was lightning in my body. Sensations built inside, storming and spinning into each other as we stared.

"I need you," Ian muttered gruffly.

Then he was spinning me around. My elbows rested on the half-wall beside the door. He shoved my jeans down roughly, just over my hips. My thighs were pressed together by the fabric, creating friction. I arched my back, crying out when he delved his fingers into my already dripping wet channel.

"Just how I need you," he murmured against the back of my neck.

He pushed my blouse up, dropping hot kisses along my spine as he fucked me with his fingers. I whimpered, pressing back into him when I felt the brush of his arousal against my bottom.

"Hang on."

I heard the sound of fabric shifting, followed by the thick press of his crown at my entrance. "Oh, God," I cried on the heels of a low moan.

He dragged the head of his cock back and forth through my folds. My voice was slurred as I begged, "Please. I need you," between broken breaths.

"Right here, darlin'."

Then he curled over me, and I felt the thick slide of him filling me. The relief was so intense, I came almost instantly. He held still inside me. I rippled around him, gulping in air as I tried to hang on to my control.

"Wait for me," he murmured.

I felt the press of his fingers on one hip, and I arched back into him when he filled me again. The stretch of it was intoxicating. Pleasure danced through me, spinning tighter and tighter. I held on for several more thrusts, and then his hand snaked around, and he did something magical with his fingers right over my clit. The pleasure finally broke through me in a crashing wave. As I cried out, I felt the heat of him filling me. He shuddered and surged into me once more.

I distantly heard him crying my name through the rush of pleasure, blocking out everything but him and this moment. I was relieved he was holding me up, and I had something to hold in front of me. Otherwise, I would have melted to the floor.

A moment later, he curled around me, resting his elbows beside mine. He brushed my hair away from my neck and pressed a lingering kiss there before murmuring, "You're gonna fucking kill me one of these days."

I laughed, the sound barely above a whisper. I felt the curve of his smile against my neck.

"We didn't even get our clothes off, Jane."

"It's not my fault. You started it," I teased.

He chuckled, the sound spinning around my heart. "I did. I thought we'd at least make it to the couch."

He straightened and slowly withdrew. I instantly missed the feel of him filling me. He was the only man who'd been with me like this, and I didn't know if it could be like that with anybody else. The intimacy of it was intense. The passion and desire and need, all of it was tangling up into emotions that were beginning to feel big and real.

I turned to face him as I righted my clothes. We stared at each other for a minute. He was buttoning his jeans, and I was shimmying mine up over my hips. It was kind of ridiculous to get dressed now.

"Let's not even bother. Let's shower," he said.

"Fine by me." I still had to tug my jeans up far enough to walk.

Ian took me by the hand and led me into the shower. Our clothes were left in a pile on the floor. He kissed me in the shower, his hands sliding over my curves with the suds. It didn't go any further, but the intimacy was almost too much.

Chapter Twenty

IAN

The following morning, I turned out to be relieved Jane left to have coffee with Thea when I got a call from the FBI office in DC.

"We're moving fast on this investigation, so you're going to see some news. Lay low and keep it quiet. We're not going to reveal your name to the press, but you might want to brace yourself for calls. There will be two arrests today," the agent explained.

"Fuck," I muttered as I leaned back into the couch cushions.

I had my laptop open and was working on some monthly reports. "It's Saturday," I replied.

"The news is quieter on the weekend," the agent replied matter-of-factly.

"They're going to assume it's me who blew the whistle," I replied.

"Probably. There are thirteen companies in the consortium, so you're one of thirteen people they're going to suspect."

"Are there other people who have given you information?" I asked. I'd asked this before, but thought maybe they'd finally answer.

"Yes, but we're not disclosing names right now."

"I understand, but it's a relief to know I'm not alone. Thanks for telling me that. Can I ask you something else?"

Chet, the agent who'd been working with me since the beginning and my main point of contact on the team, replied, "You can always ask. Doesn't mean I'll answer."

"Does my brother Dallas know anything about this?"

"He will this morning. If you want to talk to anybody, you can talk to him after we make the arrests."

I took a breath, letting it out in a slow sigh. "All right. Good to know."

"Being a whistleblower can feel lonely," Chet offered.

"No shit," I replied dryly. "How long do you think it'll be before I can talk to anyone other than my brother?"

"We'll let you know as soon as we think that's safe. The more people that know, the harder it gets to protect the information and to protect you from the fallout."

"I know, I get it."

After I got off the phone, I sighed and ran a hand through my hair. "Fuck."

I was relieved but also stressed because I knew this part of the investigation would be the most touch-and-go. There was nothing for me to do but wait it out. There would be news reports, and I didn't like keeping anything from Jane. Keeping it from my family was easier than from her.

I knew I'd fallen for her. I wanted to be able to tell her everything. There were so many unknowns right now, and I couldn't make any moves officially until this damned investigation was further along and I didn't have to worry about my involvement.

Standing, I slid my laptop onto the coffee table. I walked into the kitchen and was eyeing the almost empty coffeepot when my phone vibrated with a text.

Jane: *Should I bring a coffee home for you? This place also has yummy pastries. Do you want something sweet or something savory?*

I smiled as I looked at her text and tapped out a reply.

Me: *I'd love a coffee. Make it a strong one. I'll take sweet and savory. You pick.*

Jane: *Okay, see you in about 15 minutes. Thea says hi.*

Me: *Give her a hug for me.*

I was smiling as I returned to the living room and plunked down on the couch. I had Jane to distract me for the weekend, and she was the very best kind of distraction.

Chapter Twenty-One

JANE

Audrey's eyes took on a sly gleam as she smiled at me from across the table. Thea snickered into her coffee before taking a swallow.

"What?" I prompted, willing the heat on my cheeks to fade away.

"You and Ian are ridiculous," Thea clarified as she lowered her coffee.

"What do you mean?"

She rolled her eyes, her gaze sliding over to Audrey. "So, we had dinner last weekend when Ian was here. He hardly paid any attention to me. I think he knew I was there, but he mostly stared at Jane." She glanced back at me, lifting her shoulders in a slight shrug. "I honestly didn't think he'd ever fall for anyone. He's been such a workaholic."

"He does work a lot. Sometimes, I worry about it," I replied.

Audrey's gaze sobered. "Normal workaholic, or crazy workaholic?" she pressed.

"He's not that bad. When we spend weekends together, I grade papers, and he catches up on email and so on. He seems stressed a lot during the week, but he still texts and calls."

"How often?" Thea interjected.

Heat flared in my cheeks again, and I laughed softly as I looked her way. "We text every day, and we talk every day." I took a gulp of my coffee.

Normally, I would've gone down to DC this weekend, based on our alternating travel routine, but I'd stayed in Boston this weekend because there was an event at the college. As a newer faculty member, I didn't feel like I could bow out of it. Ian also had something going on with a case at work. For the first time in months, I wasn't seeing him on the weekend, and I missed him. I got to have coffee with two of my friends, so that was a good distraction.

Thea's laugh was sly. "You two have it bad for each other."

Audrey eyed me curiously. "I'm with Thea. I'm surprised. Not that Ian likes you. You're awesome. Just that this is really happening."

"What do you mean?"

"You two are getting serious," Audrey pointed out calmly.

My heart started beating like I had a jackrabbit in my chest, and I took a shaky breath. "You think?"

Thea let out an annoyed sigh. "If it's not obvious to you, it's obvious to everyone else. Dallas and Noah have even noticed."

I rolled my eyes. "It took me off guard too. Honestly, I haven't had a serious relationship in, well, ever."

"Ever?" Thea asked.

"I know we didn't talk that much when you were out in Seattle, but you didn't date anyone there?" Audrey added.

I shook my head. "Not seriously. It just hadn't happened. And who are you to talk?" I looked over at Audrey.

"Did you forget I was engaged before I was with Dallas? That was serious even though we broke up."

I looked at Thea whose cheeks went pink. "Fine," she muttered. "I haven't been serious with anyone."

"You were serious with Joe in high school," Audrey corrected.

"High school doesn't count," Thea said, a little too firmly in my opinion.

"You and Joe were together for over a year," Audrey offered helpfully. "I know we were young, but neither one of us had a steady boyfriend." She gestured back and forth between her and me.

I was relieved to have the focus off myself and my relationship. Some things felt unsettled and uncertain with Ian, and it terrified me to think about what that meant. I didn't even dwell because Thea looked skittish.

"Did we hit a sore spot?" I asked gently.

Thea shrugged. "No, I guess Joe and I were serious, but you know how that went." She

was twisting a napkin between her fingers.

"You never said much after high school about him," Audrey commented.

Thea shrugged. "No point."

Audrey looked at me and shrugged. I glanced at Thea. "High school is weird."

Thea nodded her head enthusiastically. "Definitely. Anyway, back to you. Maybe it's uncomfortable, but I think it's serious for him. He hasn't had a serious relationship, either. You two are going to have to stumble through this one together."

Then Audrey interjected the very question that

tumbled through my thoughts occasionally. "Have you discussed if you plan to stay where you are? You seem to be handling the long-distance thing pretty well."

"We haven't talked about that. Ian's got the business down there, and I'm here in Boston with a new position."

"That might be a conversation you should have sooner rather than later," Audrey said gently.

I took a deep breath, trying to ease the tightness in my chest. "I know."

Thea's smile was warm as she looked over at me. "I think Ian would move for you. He's talked about coming up here before anyway."

"He has?" That surprised me, although I didn't say so aloud.

"We're all here now. Except him," she replied.

A little hum of anticipation spun through me at that idea. I liked it here. I liked being near my friends, and I really liked my job so far. I wanted the option to stay here. But that definitely relied on Ian moving here if we decided to admit we wanted to take things to the next level.

Thea nudged Audrey with her elbow. "You're the only one here who knows anything about a serious relationship as an adult."

"This is stressing me out," I added

Audrey's brow furrowed when she looked over at me. "What?"

"I don't know what to do."

"You don't know what to do about what?" Thea asked as she leaned forward.

"I've never had a serious relationship, and I don't know what to think. Ian and I are doing okay with the long-distance thing, but I've been just putting off thinking about it."

Audrey pursed her lips, her gaze understanding. "Dallas and I didn't live in the same place when we first got together. Just take it one step at a time. You're here now. When the time is right, you'll know it's time to sort it out. Don't get ahead of yourself."

I took a breath and swallowed. "Okay, I won't worry about it right now."

That was a big fat lie, and Thea's lips twitched with a smile. "You're worrying."

"Stop," Audrey ordered her.

"Let's talk about something else. I've had enough talk of my relationship."

Fortunately, my old friends were still good friends, and they let the topic drop. It didn't matter, though. Later, after Ian called, all I could think about was him. I missed him. I missed his voice; I missed him being here for the weekend. I was starting to rely on him and his presence in my life. This was just one weekend when we weren't together, and I missed him so much it was a physical ache in my heart.

Chapter Twenty-Two

IAN

"How are you holding up?" my brother asked.

"Fine, I guess," I said as I turned and paced in front of the windows in my condo.

It was spring in DC, and the cherry trees were in bloom. This was one of my favorite times of the year here, yet it felt as if all I could do was pace back and forth in front of the windows and make worried calls to my brother.

"You sound stressed," Dallas replied. "Just be patient. They gave me a full update on this, and it's a solid case. Once they tie up a few more loose ends, you'll be able to stop feeling like you're keeping it to yourself. I gotta give it to you; you've handled it really well."

"It doesn't fucking feel like it," I muttered. "I don't even know how you and Noah do your jobs."

Dallas's laugh was dry. "You get used to it. Also, it's easier to hold on to information when it's not personal. You're the whistleblower in this situation, not the investigator. You also personally know the people implicated. I'm really proud of you."

Although I knew my brothers didn't think much of it, I was the youngest brother and the only one who didn't go into the FBI. Sometimes, I felt like the least responsible of the bunch even though I'd been the one to rebuild our family's decimated finances in the aftermath of our father's crimes. It meant a lot to have Dallas say he was proud of me.

Because he was apparently a fucking mind reader as well, he added, "And you know we're all grateful for what you did and still do since we lost most everything."

"Thanks, man," I said gruffly.

"How are things with Jane?" He deftly changed the subject.

My lips automatically curled into a smile because everything with Jane was good. Except for one thing— my stress with work and this stupid investigation. I didn't mention that to Dallas.

"We're good. She'll be down this weekend."

"Are you stressing out because you can't tell her what's going on with work?"

"Yeah, I don't like keeping this a secret. My work schedule has been fucking hell because of it. I've been trying to work around and rebuild the business outside of the consortium without anybody picking up on what I'm doing, but it's stressful. I want to tell her because she means a lot to me."

"You sound like a man in love," Dallas said so matter-of-factly my heart lurched unsteadily in my chest.

"Wh-What?" I sputtered.

"Just what I said. Does that freak you out?"

"Hell, yeah, that freaks me out."

Dallas laughed lightly. "You'll be fine. I think Jane is good for you."

"Really? Actually, I don't even know why I'm asking that," I corrected. "I know she's good for me."

"Then why are you freaked out about me saying you sound like you're in love?" he asked pointedly.

I shifted my shoulders uncomfortably and finally stopped my pacing. I adjusted one of my loose earbuds as I replied, "I don't know. I didn't expect any of this. I sure as hell didn't expect things to get serious."

"Is there a problem with things getting serious?" my brother pressed.

"Uh, no. It's just she's in Boston, and I'm here. I don't know..." My words trailed off, and I didn't like the discomfort around this. Sometimes, I had a hard time believing how fast this had happened with her.

It had been four months, and we'd spent all but a few weekends together. Now, I was counting down the minutes—literally glancing at my phone, the clock on the wall, and my watch repeatedly—as I waited for when I could go meet her at the train station.

"Maybe you should stop thinking so hard about it," Dallas offered.

"Ya think?" I teased lightly.

"Yeah, overthinking feelings isn't really helpful."

"Are you an expert now?"

"I don't know if I'm an expert, but more than you, I suppose."

"Damn straight. You're married, you've got a kid, and you're happy. I'm really happy for you. I'm happy for Noah too."

"It's your turn. Maybe you should move up to Boston. You've thought about it before, and that was before you and Jane got together."

"I haven't told her yet, but that's my plan eventually." I decided to be blunt with my brother.

"Seriously?"

"Yeah, but I haven't talked to her about it yet. I want to get through this whole legal case so that I can make some changes business-wise. I can't do that until the legal mess is done. If I try while it's still going on, too many questions will come up from my partners."

"Makes sense, so you'll have to wait. We'd love it if you were up here."

"I'd love to be there," I said, meaning it.

My two brothers, my sister, and I had always been close. But we'd grown apart some after our mother died. She'd been the touchstone for the whole family. And then our father obliterated what little respect we had for him. He'd been cold, distant, and occasionally cruel when we were kids. Then he'd committed massive financial fraud and landed himself in jail. In the reverberations of that, my siblings and I had pulled closer again. The idea of being in Boston with them had been blipping on my radar for a while now. Jane's presence only sweetened the idea.

———

I waited outside the train station. Whenever I came here to meet Jane, I often felt like a restless little boy. Impatience spurred me as people filtered off the train, and I peered around to catch a glimpse of her honey-gold hair. The second I saw her adjusting her backpack on her shoulders with her eyes down as she stepped off the train, my heart gave a rounding kick, and anticipation sizzled through me. What had started as pure attraction was tangling like a vine within emotion. I didn't think the two could be separated anymore.

Oh, to be sure, I *wanted* Jane. Fiercely. But it was more than that, so much more. I missed her when she wasn't here, and seeing her elicited an unfamiliar sense of joy inside. I watched, waiting for the second she would lift her head. When she did, she glanced around before pressing her glasses up on her nose, a habit that made my heart twist with a sweet ache. Her eyes arced about the area before her gaze landed on mine. Her lips curled into a smile. I was moving swiftly, threading through the crowd, until I reached her.

"Hey—" she began, her voice muffled as I wrapped her in my arms and pulled her close.

I needed to touch her. As much as she stirred deep waters inside me, only she could help me feel anchored and not set adrift on the tumult of my own stormy emotions. I breathed in the scent of her that had become familiar, a little musky with a subtle floral hint from her soap. When I lifted my head, she peered up at me.

"I missed you," she said immediately.

I brushed her hair away from her face. "I missed you too," I said gruffly.

"Are you okay?" she asked, her eyes searching mine.

I took a breath. I was, and I wasn't. I wanted to tell her everything, the bundle of stress of the last seven months or so, all of it tangled up in work and the bitterness and cynicism that I tried to avoid. I wanted to tell her it hurt me to keep this from her— even though I knew I had to until it was okay not to— yet I couldn't say any of that.

I simply answered, "I am now," because that was entirely true.

Jane was here, and we had the whole weekend together. I was getting greedy, though, and I wanted more. She leaned up and pressed a kiss along the edge of my jaw. I angled down, catching her lips with mine. Right there in the train station with people surrounding us, I fit my mouth over hers and got lost in a fiery hot kiss. I held her close and took deep sips from her mouth. The sound of someone calling something snapped through my awareness, and we broke apart.

Jane's cheeks were tinged pink, and her eyes bashful. "Wow," she said.

"I did say I missed you," I offered with a grin. "Want me to carry your bag?"

She shook her head. "It's a backpack, and I'm already wearing it."

We turned, and I caught her hand, lacing my fingers through hers. Once we started walking, I prompted, "Tell me how your week was." I'd grown to love this time when we were connected. These moments were mundane, but I loved just catching up. The time was sweetened because I didn't have her all week, so it was nice. I thought about my conversation with Dallas.

Even though there were things I couldn't tell her, I wanted to share with her my eventual plan to move to Boston. I told myself I would when the time was right. A few minutes later, we were in the car, and Jane said, "Let's get takeout and just stay in tonight."

I slid my gaze to hers as I waited at a stoplight. "Yeah?"

Her teeth snagged her bottom lip, and she nodded quickly. "Do you want to call now?"

"What do you want for takeout?"

I rolled my eyes. "You know me. I'm easy when it comes to food. What do *you* want?"

She grinned. "How about Indian food? That place we went to a few weeks ago."

"Sounds good. You can order for me."

I drove while she called in our order, and we picked it up on the way to my place. The weekend started out good, *really* good. For some reason, I held back on mentioning my plan to move to Boston because I didn't know when. The "when" of it was important. If this legal case dragged on too long, I might need to be down here longer than I hoped. Maybe I could just say fuck it and leave, but I wasn't ready to consider that yet. Everything was good up until late Saturday afternoon.

Then I got a call from the investigator. Jane was grading papers, so I took the call in the room I used for an office in my condo when I wanted to work from home. "What's up?" I asked by way of greeting.

"Well, I thought I should give you a heads-up that we've gotten calls from two of the other whistleblowers. One of the targets has gotten wind of the investigation and is trying to figure out who talked to us. I think you should be prepared for him to call. I know we've already discussed what you should say, but do you need to run through it again?"

Tension coiled in my gut, mingling with a bitter acid of dread. "I'm all set. I know exactly what I need to say, and I'm not going to take his call. I'll handle it."

"Good idea. Keep me posted with any updates."

"You do the same."

"Fuck," I said to myself as I lowered my phone.

I'd been hoping all this time that I would just be able to tell Jane what was going on before the tension twisted between us. Now, I was going to have to do my damnedest to keep this tension from being obvious. I managed it for the rest of the weekend, but I was distracted. I knew she sensed it. The only time I wasn't distracted was when I was making love to Jane. Thank fuck, that was one place where my escape was complete. Elemental and pure, nothing could slip into my consciousness once Jane and I were skin to skin.

But Sunday, when I took her to the train station, she looked over at me. "Are you okay?"

"Yeah, fine," I said quickly, probably a little too quickly.

Her eyes searched mine. "Okay. Would you tell me if you weren't?"

Chapter Twenty-Three

JANE

Of course, I would.

Ian's answer repeated in my thoughts. I didn't know how I knew, but I knew he wasn't telling me something. Something that was causing a lot of stress for him. That awareness felt like a little paper cut in my consciousness, in my trust for him, or rather, in my trust for our relationship.

Whatever was going on was creating a constant sense of tension. Every time he spoke, I could hear it in his voice. Yet every time I asked, he assured me he was fine. I didn't mind someone keeping me out. I also respected that we all had to keep our own counsel and keep corners of ourselves entirely private.

None of it would matter, except I'd fallen in love with him. Talk about a complication I hadn't expected. Meanwhile, my parents' house was officially on the market, and the real estate agent was bombarding my parents with questions. They'd already had several offers. If the financing came through for one of them, the place where I'd grown up would belong to another family. This should *not* be a big deal. Not at all.

Except visiting Haven's Bay had brought back so many memories, and I loved my little hometown. If the house sold and things didn't work out with Ian, I wouldn't have any excuse to visit anymore.

Dammit. Now, that felt too emotional. I spun in my desk chair to look out the windows. My office had a slice of a view of the Charles River. It was late afternoon, and people were running, walking, and biking along the path beside the river. The weather was getting nicer and summer was on the horizon.

I decided to put my worries out of my thoughts and assume things were okay. Whatever was bothering Ian probably had something to do with work and nothing to do with me. I wanted to be one of those couples walking along the river where we'd stop and get takeout and then go home together. Of course, that spun into another little paper cut of a worry. Small but stinging.

If we were going to be serious, we couldn't do this long-distance thing forever. Maybe we could, but that wasn't what I wanted. Restless, I spun back around in my chair and decided it was time to go. I saved what I'd been working on to my laptop. I'd grade the rest of the papers when I got home tonight and upload everything to the online system. Meanwhile, I'd walk myself along the Charles River and get my own takeout for dinner. That was more appealing than staying late in my office.

———

"There," I said to myself after I finished grading the last midterm paper.

As I leaned back into the couch cushions, my eyes landed on the clock on my phone. It was nine o'clock at night, and I still hadn't had an evening call from Ian. This was unusual.

I flicked on the television, scanning the channels before settling on a home renovation show. I'd never owned my own house, but I liked the idea. Not that I could do my own remodeling, but I loved painting. The repetition of it was soothing for me.

I knew I could call Ian myself, but for some reason, I was holding back. When I realized I'd lifted my phone and checked the time for the third time inside of fifteen minutes, I sighed and swiped my thumb across the screen, immediately pulling up his number and calling him. Because I was being stupid.

Ian picked up on the first ring. "Hey, Jane. Sorry, I meant to call you sooner."

He sounded tired and stressed. "Busy with work?" I prompted, my heart twinging with empathy.

"I am, but that's no excuse. How was your day?"

"Pretty good. Doing midterm grading, so that's always fun. I'm feeling ahead of the curve, though. Aside from work bogging you down, how are things?"

"It's all work for me this week."

"Did you at least eat more than that bagel?" I teased lightly. He'd texted me a photo of the bagel he'd picked up this morning on his way to the office.

"I did, I promise."

"Do you know what time you'll be getting here this Friday?"

"Should be by seven. Will that work?"

"Of course. Text me what you want for dinner, and I'll pick it up before you get here."

"You got it."

There was a longer than usual pause before I

cleared my throat. "Well, I'll let you get back to work. Make sure you get some sleep tonight, okay?"

His low laugh sounded tired, and my heart twisted with worry. "I will. Talk to you tomorrow."

"Good night."

The words "I love you" hovered in my throat, almost a visceral presence, but I held back. Not because I didn't know how I felt. It's just we hadn't gotten to that stage yet. I felt a pinch of worry in my chest as I lowered the phone to my lap.

He sounded downright weary, and I wished I knew why work was so stressful. I knew from before we'd reconnected over the holidays that he was a busy guy. He ran an investment company, one he'd started himself in the aftermath of everything blowing up with their father and his business. I imagined he worked long hours. As it was, I worked plenty of hours myself. Now that I was on a tenure track, I knew I would be staying busy.

Of course, that train of thought immediately rounded back to what would happen if we decided to really commit and figure out who was going to move. I flung my phone on the couch cushion beside me, shaking my head as I tucked my feet under my hips. A minute later, I stood from the couch and crossed into the kitchen to pour myself a glass of wine. I needed to relax, not obsess about Ian.

When I spoke to him Thursday, he sounded better, more like himself, without that thread of tension. Friday, he texted me in the afternoon to say he'd love some takeout from one of our favorite Thai restaurants.

I was walking to pick it up when my phone vibrated in my pocket. Sliding it out, Ian's name flashed on the screen. I answered immediately.

"Hey, Jane. I'm glad I caught you."

"What's up?"

The sound of him inhaling sharply filtered through the phone. "Look, I'm not gonna make it tonight."

I reflexively glanced at my watch, my feet coming to a stop. Someone walking behind me skirted around. I stepped to the edge of the sidewalk, stopping to lean against a brick building.

"Is everything okay?"

"Yeah, it'll be fine. I've got a problem at work, dealing with some stuff. I won't be focused if I come up."

This was odd, if only because I didn't see how he couldn't have known this only a few hours earlier. After a brief pause, I opened my mouth to tell him I wouldn't mind if he worked all weekend here. Because I missed him, and I wanted to see him. I didn't say any of that.

"Oh," I finally said.

"Rain check for next weekend? I'll come up there, I promise," he said.

"Oka-aay." I heard myself saying slowly. An uncomfortable sense of uncertainty was unspooling inside.

"I miss you," he said quickly. "I'm really sorry."

"It's okay, I understand." I tried to force some lightness into my tone, but I knew my words were coming out stilted, and my throat felt tight. "I miss you too."

"I'll call you tomorrow."

"All right. Good night," I said, trying to force my tone to sound casual.

I hung up quickly. I pushed away from the building and began walking as I slid my phone in my pocket and adjusted my purse where the strap was angled across my chest. I decided to get that Thai takeout anyway. I was starving, and I'd rather have that than try to scramble up something on my own at home. That would only make me feel even lonelier.

Chapter Twenty-Four

JANE

"What do you mean he's not here?" Thea asked.

I adjusted the phone on my shoulder as I turned off the faucet with one hand and quickly dried my hands. A moment later, I gripped the phone in my hand again. "He said something came up with work. He didn't say what."

"And you didn't ask?" Thea pressed.

"No," I muttered, feeling a little foolish. "Do you know something about what's going on?"

I hated that I was quizzing his sister for answers and, even more so, that I'd felt like I couldn't ask Ian.

"No, he's always been a workaholic, but that's kind of weird for him to cancel like that without explaining. You two have been visiting every weekend, right?"

"Yeah," I said quickly.

"Well, I think you should ask him when he calls. His job is his job, but you're more important," Thea offered pointedly.

"Okay, okay. I will. Sometimes it's hard to focus on work when you're trying to do other things," I offered.

I was trying really hard to be understanding and

make sense of it, but the whole thing felt weird, and I didn't know why. It made me feel like something else was going on with him, and he just wasn't telling me. Maybe it had something to do with me. I didn't say any of that to Thea. She was his sister, and I wasn't going to get into that with her.

"If you find out what's up, tell me. I'm also going to call him and do a little reconnaissance for you. I'll fill you in."

"Thea," I warned. "Don't you dare. That's ridiculous."

"Why is it ridiculous?" she countered. "He's my brother, so I can be as nosy as I want."

"But I don't want him to think I'm asking you to do that."

My friend let out a sharp, dry laugh. "He would never think that. I'm nosy anyway," she said flatly.

I laughed because that was entirely true. "I'll talk to you soon."

"Don't make it more than it is," she added.

"Okay. I won't," I said, rolling my eyes even though she couldn't see me.

After I got off the phone, I settled into grading more papers.

Audrey called to check in with me as well. Even when she invited me to meet her for lunch, I demurred. Not because I didn't want to see her, but she was married to Ian's brother. It felt like a little merry-go-round of too many people connected and me feeling foolish about all of it. I told myself it was nothing. I told myself I would be fine. I was. Until I got a phone call from a reporter.

IAN

"They called my girlfriend," I said flatly, trying not to let my anger ramp up.

The prosecutor shrugged. "I did not give them your girlfriend's name, or phone number, or contact information. I don't even have it to give. The reality is once people start nosing around, they start making phone calls. One of the guys is willing to make a plea deal, and they must have talked to somebody. We can't keep a lid on what others say or do."

"Fuck," I muttered, leaning back in the chair and drumming my fingertips on the table.

"I'm sorry," the prosecutor said. "It's blown wide open."

"Am I allowed to talk to her about it now?" I asked. I didn't even bother to keep the sarcasm out of my tone.

He nodded. "You are."

"Do you need me this afternoon for anything?"

"Don't think so. We'll keep you posted on any developments."

"Got it." I stood quickly and left the office.

I had my phone out of my pocket as soon as I was in the hallway. Jane didn't answer.

"Fuck," I muttered to myself as I listened to her voicemail.

"Jane, it's me. I understand you got a call from a reporter. If I'd known this was blowing up, I would have given you a heads-up. I have no idea how they got your name or your phone number. I'm really sorry. Please call me."

I ended that call, immediately jabbing at my screen to call Dallas next.

He answered immediately. "How're you holding up?"

"I'm fine. A fucking reporter got Jane's name and number and called her."

Dallas groaned. "That sucks. At least everything's out in the open now. It's all over the news already."

"I don't give a shit about that. I mean, I do," I corrected. "But Jane didn't answer when I tried to call her."

"I'll ask Audrey to try to reach out to her," Dallas offered. "She's probably working now, right?"

"Fuck, fuck," I muttered.

"I'm sure she'll understand."

"I hope so. I wanted to tell her, and I canceled last weekend. Now there's no way I'm going up there. If reporters are looking for her, they're gonna look for me. I'll just end up bringing them to her doorstep. I don't want to fucking do that."

I ran my free hand through my hair, feeling ragged with my nerves strung tight.

"It'll blow over," my brother said, his tone calm and soothing. "There's going to be a little explosion in phone calls, but just dial down your stress and wait. All you can do is wait this out. The FBI will field most of this for you."

"I hope so. I'll keep trying to call Jane. If Audrey is able to get ahold of her, please let me know right away."

"You got it," Dallas replied.

After that call, I walked briskly down the hallway and jabbed at the elevator button when I reached the bank of elevators. After too many minutes passed, I swore and jogged to the stairs. I was too restless to stand around waiting. Moments later, I walked outside of the building, glancing around quickly before aiming for home. I was tempted to go to my office, but I figured I'd be more likely to encounter reporters there.

I spent the afternoon trying to reach Jane and fielding phone calls from nosy reporters. All three of the guys involved in the scam had been arrested. All three pled not guilty this afternoon and were released on bond. Meanwhile, I just wanted to talk to Jane.

She finally answered. "Hi," she said, her tone almost impossible to read in that one word,

"Jane, thank God." I let out a heavy sigh. "Did you get my message?"

"I did. It's okay."

Relief rushed through me. "I'm sorry. I have no idea how they got your name or your number."

"It's fine. I just wish you had told me what was going on."

"I couldn't." A sense of unease chased through me.

"Oh no, I understand you couldn't tell me about the case. But maybe telling me something serious was going on that you couldn't tell me about for legal reasons would have been nice."

"Jane." I paused, leaning my head back into the

couch cushions and sliding my laptop onto the coffee table. "Okay. I guess I could have said that, but I didn't know the best way to handle it." When she didn't say anything, I asked, "What did the reporter want?"

"They wanted to know what I knew and if I thought you were involved in it. I just told them I didn't know because that was the truth. I didn't even know what they were asking about."

"I'm not involved in *any* of it, Jane. I stumbled across this, and I turned into a fucking whistleblower. It's been going on for months, and it sucks. That's why I was up in Haven's Bay in December. I needed a break from the pressure. I wasn't allowed to talk to anyone, not even Dallas and Noah. Even though they work for the FBI, this case is not under their jurisdiction. It was on lockdown."

"I understand, Ian. I really do," she said quietly.

"Are you upset with me?" I asked, even though I was almost afraid to ask.

Jane was silent just long enough that dread churned in my gut. "I'm not upset that you couldn't talk to me about this. I totally understand. You literally couldn't. But maybe a clue, maybe just tell me something really screwed up is going on at work. I don't know. I think maybe I'm taking this more seriously than you are."

Oh, fuck.

"Jane. No, you're not. I promise."

"I don't mean the case, but what it meant for you not to say anything, anything at all, about something."

"Jane—"

"Let's take a couple of weekends off. I'm sure you need to stay put with everything going on with that case."

That dread churned into panic. "Actually, I don't.

They don't need anything from me right now. I'll just be playing dodgeball with reporters who are nosy about what's going on."

"I don't really want to play dodgeball with reporters either, so it's probably best for you to handle them."

"What do you mean you're taking us more seriously than me?" I asked, my brain finally catching up to the important part of what she said.

"What do you think I mean? I didn't plan for any of this. Okay? I didn't mean to fall for you, but I did. You're Thea's brother, and it's starting to feel messy. With everything going on, let's take a break. We'll talk soon. Bye."

"Jane, I really—"

The phone line had gone dead in my ear. I was about to call again, but my fingers hovered over the screen.

"Fuck, fuck, fuck," I muttered to my empty apartment.

I called Dallas, and he answered immediately. "What's up?"

"Jane wants a break," I said without preamble. "Could I have talked to her about this sooner?"

"Talk to her about what?"

"The case. She said that she wished I'd mentioned something was going on at work that was really stressing me out. But could I have told her there was a legal issue? They told me I couldn't talk to anyone, not even you and Noah."

"That's right," Dallas said slowly. "You talking to anyone could have created problems. It's good you didn't. Was it against the law? No, I mean whistle-blowers talk to people all the time. You're not an agent on the case. They are. They asked you not to say anything because they were worried about things blowing up. You did the right thing. In my experience, saying anything only leads to questions. You've been sitting on this for months. How do you feel?"

"I don't even care about the stupid case. I didn't say anything because I didn't want to be that jerk who was all vague. Fuck, I miss her."

"Of course, you do. Things are far enough along with her. At some point, somebody's got to make a move."

"What do you mean, make a move?"

"Either you let it come to a natural conclusion, or you tell her how you feel."

"I already told you my plan was to come up there. I was waiting for this case to be done so I could wrap things up here with my business so it didn't look weird."

"I know, but did you mention that to her?" he asked, too pointedly in my opinion.

"Uh, no," I said slowly, feeling foolish. Should I call her and tell her that right now? Right after she said she wanted a break?"

"I don't know. I think you need to let her know how you feel. If you love her, she should know."

I sighed. "This sucks. You could've told me that sooner."

"Did you know you loved her?"

"I hadn't really thought it through. I just..." My words petered out, and I felt even more foolish.

Dallas chuckled. "All right, slick, you'll figure this out."

"Don't fucking call me slick." That was Dallas's old nickname for me, although he hadn't used it in years.

Back when I was in high school, the nickname fit

for the very guy Jane dismissed while I barely noticed her. "I'm not that guy anymore," I added.

"I know you're not. But Jane is the first woman you've been serious about," he said, his tone shifting from teasing to somber.

"I know. Maybe you should call Thea. She and Jane are friends, so she might have some advice."

I groaned while Dallas chuckled in response. "Nice chatting," he offered right before we ended the call.

Taking a deep breath and letting it out, I leaned forward and rested my elbows on my knees. I idly stared down at my phone screen. Calling my sister meant I needed to be prepared. She would have an opinion. First, I needed to eat because I was fucking starving, and I could hardly think straight at this point.

Chapter Twenty-Six

JANE

"You told him you needed a break?" Audrey prompted.

"Yeah, just—" I paused abruptly and rolled my shoulders back to ease the tension tightening between my shoulder blades. "Audrey, I've had four reporters call me inside of an hour. I feel like I'm flying blind. He knew this whole thing was going on, way back when we got together over Christmas."

"It's not like he could tell you he was a whistle-blower on a major investigation."

"Well, he could have said something big was happening that he couldn't talk to me about."

"At first?" My friend eyed me skeptically.

"Well, no, but when we started getting serious."

"I get being frustrated, but Ian was in a tight spot. He was a whistleblower against three people with lots of money. They've been criminally charged with felonies, and they're looking at serious time. He's lucky he's not the only whistleblower, so it takes some pressure off. I'm not sure you could expect him to say something. I know I'd have asked questions if he tried to be all vague."

"I know." I sighed, my shoulders sagging with it. "I feel like I'm emotionally ahead of him."

"Because you love him? Have you told him how you felt?"

"No. Are you insane?"

"Last I checked, no," Audrey offered dryly.

I let out another sigh. "I know you're not crazy. It's just—" I paused abruptly, taking a gulp of my coffee. "We're still pretty fresh."

"What do you mean by fresh?"

"I mean, what started out as just—"

"A holiday fling," Audrey interjected helpfully when I stuttered over what to say.

I laughed. "Okay, a holiday fling. And now, I don't think either one of us planned on this. I don't even know how fast relationships are supposed to move."

"I don't think there are rules on that. I think if he was brand new to you and you didn't know him, four months would be different. But you've been spending every weekend together. And it's not like you haven't known him for—"

This time, she paused, and I interjected, "As long as I can remember. We weren't exactly close when we were younger, though."

That got me a hard eye roll. "We all hung out together all the time. He was one of Thea's older brothers. My point is, he's not a stranger. We know he's not a secret serial killer by now."

I threw my hands up in the air and glared at her. "I know he's not a secret serial killer. But he had this major thing happening, and I didn't know about it."

"He couldn't tell you," she said, leaning forward.

"He could have told me something was going on."

"And then what? You'd have had questions. I see your point. It's just where was that conversation supposed to go? It's a weird situation. That's all I'm saying. But it's obvious you really have feelings for him, and I hate to see you throw this away."

"I know. I do have feelings for him," I murmured. "It's just I felt like he was out of my league anyway."

"Why is he out of your league?" Audrey asked, her tone almost sharp.

"You knew what he was like in high school. He was handsome and popular with girls chasing after him."

My friend gave me a searching look. "I'm not going to argue the point that Ian was handsome. Obviously, he was and is. But that doesn't make him out of your league."

"I think I'm still hung up that I was pretty much the opposite of him in high school. It's hard to believe he wants to be with me now when he barely noticed me then."

"Well, believe it. You're beautiful, you're smart, and you're totally a catch. Trust me. These are facts."

"If I am such a catch, how come no one else noticed before?"

Audrey's brows hitched as she gave me a considering look. "Because you don't give anybody a chance, and maybe you just didn't meet the right guy. Plus, men are stupid sometimes."

I laughed. "Fine then."

"I think you should call Ian. Stop letting this get in the way."

I wrinkled my nose and sighed. "I'll think about it."

"Dallas thinks Ian's in love with you." I almost choked on a swallow of water. Audrey continued, "Actually, he doesn't think. He said he knows it."

"How could he know?" I managed.

"He knows Ian well. They're all close. They've gotten really tight these past few years. They lost their mom, and they got even closer in the aftermath of what happened with their dad. They talk all the time."

Just then, Audrey glanced at her watch. "Oh, I need to go. I've got a meeting at work."

I stood from the table as she did. "It's good to see you. Thanks for listening."

Her smile was warm. "Always. I'm so glad you're in Boston now."

She left with a smile and a wave. I promised her we'd have lunch soon. Her parting comment about me being in Boston had me mulling over it. Living hours apart was no small barrier to Ian and me.

I finished my coffee and walked back toward the university, only to encounter a reporter.

"Ma'am, can you tell us what you knew about Ian Tate being the primary whistleblower on the finance case?"

Ugh. I hated that the case was all over the news. "No comment," I said firmly.

"Surely, you knew something about this," the reporter countered.

"Actually, you probably know more than I do," I said, my tone a little too sharp.

I'd had to field phone calls, so having a reporter thrust a phone in my face with another reporter holding a camera left me feeling unsettled.

"We understand you're an old family friend. Do you think it's possible Ian was involved in the scam himself? Like father, like son."

I *knew* that was bullshit, but I pressed my lips together and took a breath. "Of course not," I said swiftly. "Now, if you'll excuse me."

I hurried past them, relieved to reach the main entrance of the building where my office was at the university. I jogged up the stairs, closing and locking my door before sitting down at my desk with a giant sigh. I didn't have time to dwell. I had three classes in a row. For that, I was relieved. I didn't need to be obsessing about it this afternoon.

Chapter Twenty-Seven

IAN

My jaw was clenched tight as I watched the brief interaction with a reporter and Jane on the evening news. They included that little snippet as part of a story on the overall case.

"Fuck my life," I muttered to myself.

As soon as the segment was over, I called Dallas. He answered with, "I just saw. It'll pass."

"What the fuck? I cannot believe they're insinuating that somehow I'm a part of this."

"They just want clicks and eyeballs. That's it. Just ignore it. You've opened up the books, and the case is rock solid. I talked to the main investigator who's handling it today. They've already got two of the guys involved working on plea deals. That will tighten up their case against the main instigator of the whole situation. Just be patient. The media will get bored soon."

"Should I call Jane?"

"Of course, you should call Jane. Why are you even asking me that?" Dallas retorted.

"Because she hasn't returned my messages."

"Ah, well then. For once, maybe you're going to have to chase her."

"What are you implying?"

"I didn't mean that in a bad way. Just that you haven't been serious with anyone, and you've not had a shortage of women willing to go along with a no-strings kind of arrangement. You've known Jane since we were kids. It's obvious to me that you love her—"

I cut in, "I already said I did."

"So you did. Jane probably feels confused and doesn't know what to think. Like I said already, maybe you should tell her you're planning to eventually move to Boston. Because maybe she's thinking, why bother dealing with all this if it can't go anywhere anyway?"

I took a breath, letting it out in a ragged sigh. "Good point. I'll try again."

This time when I called Jane, she actually answered. I was so surprised I almost didn't know what to say.

She prompted, "Ian, I'm here."

I dived right in. "I'm sorry about the media. I know you're getting calls, and I'm really sorry that they approached you today."

"It's okay. Obviously, none of that is your responsibility. I can imagine you're fending off more than I am."

"I'm in the middle of it, and now you're caught up in it. It's like a riptide, and I wish people would leave you alone."

"I'm not sure who figured out I was an old family friend," she said.

"People are nosy, and it's not hard to find out you're from Haven's Bay. Look, I know this is weird, and you feel like I hid something from you, but I need to tell you something." I took a breath, trying to ignore the twisty feeling in my belly. I'd never told anyone I was in love with them. I told her I missed her all the time, but it wasn't the same. "I'm planning to move to Boston."

"You are?" she squeaked.

She sounded so surprised I couldn't help but laugh. "Oh, yes. I'd been thinking about it before you and I connected. I didn't have a timeframe. I also didn't want to make a move on it until this case situation was dealt with. I was concerned how that would look since my company is part of the overall consortium. My long-term plan is to keep an office here, but I'll mostly work there. I can travel down here when I need to. I may eventually completely relocate. It's not like I have to stay in one place."

Jane was quiet for several beats. Uncertainty, which I fucking hated, slid through me.

"Jane?" I finally prompted.

"I'm here," she replied, her tone low.

"Is it okay that I'm planning to move there eventually?"

"Of course, it's okay."

"I miss you." I paused and took a careful breath. "I wasn't sure where things stood with us because we didn't really talk about it. This whole case blew up, and I know it's a little crazy. I'm sorry I didn't tell you something was going on. I didn't want to lie. I didn't know how to explain, and maybe that wasn't the best call."

"It's okay. I understand."

She fell quiet again, and I felt pressed to ask, "Is it okay? How are you feeling about me moving up there?"

"I'd love that."

My phone vibrated against my ear, and I lifted it

away. The name for my main contact on the investigation flashed on the screen, but I refused to answer it just now.

"I can't come up this weekend, but would you be able to come here?"

"I think so," Jane replied. "I'll text you by Friday. Will that work?"

"Sure." I was disappointed that she didn't confirm immediately, but I would be patient. "I miss you. I hope I'll see you this weekend."

After the call, I realized I hadn't told her I loved her. I wanted to call her back, but I also didn't want to call her back. Because I needed to see her face when I told her how I felt.

Chapter Twenty-Eight

JANE

Thea stared at me, her lips twisting to the side. "Okay, I have tried to stay out of this, but you're being stupid," she said pointedly.

"What do you mean?" I ground out.

"You're in love with Ian, and he's in love with you. Now, just go fucking see him. Or maybe, communicate your feelings. I don't know."

I stared at her. Obviously for too long because she circled her hand in the air impatiently.

"Just admit I'm right. You're miserable. He's a stress ball."

"He is?"

"He said he talked to you yesterday." One brow rose in an arch as my friend eyed me. "I would think you would know that."

I sighed. "You're right. I guess I didn't expect this."

My heart pinched in my chest. Merely thinking about the level of stress he was under and, suddenly, all of my worries softened. I couldn't imagine how stressful this was for him. Thea was right.

"You're right," I announced. I knew Thea well

enough to know she liked to be told when she was right.

She practically beamed. "I know I am. Now, I think the ball's in your court."

"Why is it in my court?"

"Look, I'm not going to pretend I'm an expert at romance because I'm not. But you're the one who got upset and wanted some space. Logically, you're the one who has to fix this. My brother's not perfect. I mean, my God, he used to be so annoying." I choked back a laugh as she continued, "But he's a good guy. With everything that happened with our dad, this is like stress times a thousand. You need to make him feel better."

———

Normally, my train ride down to Washington, DC, was productive. I worked and stayed focused. I got plenty of those small, tedious tasks done. Today, I wasn't focused. I was impatient.

I'd almost considered driving, but then I realized that was pointless because driving definitely wasn't going to get me there faster. My fingers kept twitching. I wanted to text him and tell him I was coming, but I also wanted to surprise him.

Restless, I drummed my fingers on the seat and kept crossing and uncrossing my legs. Eventually, the man sitting beside me glanced my way. He was an older man with kind blue eyes. "How're you doing over there?" he asked with a slight smile.

"I'm fine. Sorry." I laced my fingers together in my lap.

"No need to apologize. What are you doing in DC for the weekend?"

"Visiting my boyfriend."

"Well, then, I hope you have a good weekend."

"How about you? What brings you from Boston to DC?"

He was quiet for a few beats and his smile faded. "I wish I was your age and visiting my girlfriend, although this train wasn't here back in those days."

"Oh?" I queried, my curiosity piqued.

"I used to work in politics. I wasn't a politician, but I worked in DC for many years. I met my wife there. She was a reporter."

"Where is she now?" As soon as that question came out, I realized it was the wrong question.

The man's eyes softened. "She's not with the world anymore, but I miss her every day."

"I'm so sorry," I said hurriedly.

His smile was wistful this time. "Thank you. I can't complain. We were married for almost sixty years. I don't know what's going on with you and your boyfriend, or if he's the man for you. Everything with romance is different these days. People meet on the computer or their phone. I don't even understand that. But if you love him and he's a good man, it's worth it."

I mulled those words over after I got off the train. It was only then I realized I'd forgotten to plan how I was getting from here to Ian's condo. He usually picked me up.

I pulled up a car service app when I heard, "Jane."

Ian's voice felt like a light tap on my heart, sending a ripple through my entire system. Spinning around, I found him approaching on the sidewalk. My hand flew to my chest when he stopped in front of me, his smile wide.

"Hey there."

"How did you know I would be here?"

"Thea told me. Actually, she didn't know for sure, but she thought you might be here. I decided to chance it and come find you. No need to order a ride."

My eyes stung with salty tears, and my throat felt suddenly tight. A sense of intense emotion and joy rose swiftly. His hands were in his pockets when he stepped closer, leaning down until his forehead rested against mine.

"I forgot to mention something when we talked yesterday." His voice was low, the sound of it vibrating through me.

I swallowed. "You did?"

"I love you."

My breath caught in my throat, and I was frozen for a moment. It wasn't exactly a shock. More as if I needed that moment to absorb the words and the meaning contained within them. When I could breathe again, I whispered, "I love you too."

My voice was thick with tears. He lifted his head slightly, his eyes searching mine. He swiped one tear and then another away from my cheeks with his thumb. "I didn't mean to make you cry."

I shook my head, taking a sniffling breath and dragging my sleeve inelegantly across my nose. "It's just a lot of feeling. Not bad, though."

Then he was wrapping his arms around me and holding me tight. I tucked my head into the curve of his neck and breathed him in.

Chapter Twenty-Nine

IAN

It felt beyond good to have Jane back in my arms. It had only been weeks, but damn, I had missed her so much. I cataloged the feel of her, every little detail—her subtle scent, her softness against me, the little sound she made in her throat when my palm moved up and down her back in a soothing pass, and the raspy sound of her voice when she murmured, "I missed you."

She leaned back to peer up at me, precisely when my phone vibrated in my pocket. It was in my shirt pocket, so she felt it.

"Should you get that?" she prompted when I ignored it through three entire vibration cycles.

"Not right now."

"What if—?"

I cut her off, putting a finger over her lips. "I don't care if it's something about that damn case. I've done my part. Now, come on, let's go back to my place. We can get takeout for dinner on the way."

Because of our habit of traveling on the weekends,

I'd grown to love getting takeout with her. It meant it was just us.

She adjusted her backpack on her shoulders, and I reached for her hand, lacing my fingers through hers as we walked to my car.

As much as I wanted the weekend to be just us, it wasn't. I was inundated with phone calls as the main players were working on a plea deal. There were more reporter calls and calls from the other companies involved in the consortium. Meanwhile, I finally set in motion concrete plans to move to Boston. Nothing would be public, not for now. My lease was up on this condo in six months, which meant I could be moving up to Boston in the fall, my favorite time of the year.

"What do you think about a weekend in Haven's Bay soon?" I asked as we lay in the darkness later that night.

I had just gotten my breath back after Jane and I both went flying. With all the tumult of late, I craved the touchstone of Haven's Bay. I needed it with Jane.

"That sounds perfect. Where should we stay?"

"My family's place."

"Is that a thing we can do whenever? Do you need to check with your siblings?"

"I guess I'll let them know I'm going, but that's about it."

I could feel the curve of her smile against my shoulder where her head rested. She pressed a kiss to my collarbone, and warmth radiated in spirals from that point.

"Okay, I'll take a weekend in Haven's Bay anytime," she whispered.

EPILOGUE

Jane

"No, you can't come up this weekend," Ian said into the phone.

I snorted into my coffee cup as I lifted it to take a swallow. Ian looked up from where he was talking on his phone to Thea.

"Next weekend is fine. This weekend is out of the question."

"Are you already there?" Thea's reply carried to me.

"Yes, we are, and we'd like the house to ourselves, please," he said.

Rather firmly, I thought.

"It's not even Christmas yet for three weeks. Why are you there now?" Thea pressed.

When I glanced askance at Ian, I realized he had the phone on speaker.

"Oh, my god," he muttered. "Because this is the weekend that we came up last year."

"Oh, all right," my friend said with a dramatic sigh. "I'll be there next weekend. If you're still there, you'll have extra company."

"Love you, Thea!" I called.

"Same," she replied in return.

"Bye, sis, talk to you soon."

Ian hung up and looked across the table at me. "I should've thought to warn all of my siblings away."

"Nobody else is coming. It's not Christmas for three weeks as Thea just pointed out."

"We're not going to worry about it this weekend," he said.

He leaned across the table, catching my free hand in his. "Where do you want to have dinner tonight?"

"Emile's? They do have the best food in town."

"They do," he agreed. "We need to make a grocery store run too."

We swiveled to look out the windows. It was clear and bitingly cold outside. The wind ruffled the waters of Haven's Bay, visible through the back window. Snow covered the landscape, although it wasn't too deep yet.

We'd risen in the early hours of dawn in Boston and driven up here. Dallas and Audrey had been here over Thanksgiving, leaving some coffee for us, but the rest of the grocery situation was looking thin.

"Let's do it. We can stock up on groceries and then maybe go for a walk along the beach."

We'd fallen into the habit of coming up here on the weekends at least once a month ever since Ian moved up to Boston in September. We'd enjoyed several glorious autumn weekends here. The windowsill replacement project was almost complete. He had a goal this weekend to finish it.

The day flew by, and our walk on the beach didn't last too long even though we both had the winter gear for the weather. The wind was too much. If the sky was clear, that usually meant a windy day on the coast of Maine. We returned to the house and started a fire in the massive fireplace in the living room.

By evening, clouds had started to gather in the sky, and snow was predicted before midnight. Snow or not, we were going to have that dinner. The heels of my boots echoed on the stairs as I jogged down to the foyer.

I paused on the bottom step, my heart shifting into a thundering beat in my chest and my breath catching. He was so handsome. It was kind of ridiculous. I'd never believed my breath could be stolen by nothing more than a look. Ian could do that effortlessly.

His green eyes held mine, darkening as I finally moved, taking that last step and crossing the foyer to him. "Ready?"

He held my coat up, and I slipped my arms into the sleeves, shrugging it over my shoulders and zipping it before replying, "Now, I am."

When his lips kicked up in a half-grin, my belly tumbled, and I took a quick breath. We were just having dinner, but for some reason, I was nervous. Anticipation was humming through my body. Maybe it was because it had been a full year since he'd reentered my life.

I felt as if I was standing on the edge of something. Something big.

IAN

It was just dinner, or that was what I kept telling myself. Sherry was laughing at something Jane said. After filling our water glasses, she had taken our orders and had the menus in hand.

She glanced at me. "I'll be right back with your

drinks."

"Thanks, Sherry," I called as she hurried away, pausing to check on the table beside us.

Jane took a swallow of her water and looked across the table at me. She must have sensed my nervousness because her smile faded. "What is it?"

I cleared my throat. I had a plan—the plan involved having dinner, me staying calm, and then asking her to marry me when we got home tonight. The anticipation was driving me mad though, and I'd slipped the ring box into my jacket pocket this evening when I was getting ready.

Now, I could feel an almost literal burn in that pocket. So much for being suave and cool and keeping it together. I reached for my water, the cool glass against my fingertips doing next to nothing to abate the heat racing through me.

"Nothing," I finally replied.

Her brow furrowed. "Are you sure?"

Now, I was annoyed, not with her but with myself. "Of course, I'm sure. We're having dinner at one of our favorite places, and we're in Haven's Bay. What could be wrong?"

Jane rested her elbows on the table, giving me a long look. "I don't know. You just seem kind of weird."

I looked away, chuckling softly. Maybe my plan had fallen apart, but I could be decisive when the occasion called for it. This moment did.

I twisted slightly, reaching into my jacket where it hung on the back of my chair to fetch the small, silk-covered box. When I met her gaze again, she had a casual, almost teasing glint in her eyes.

As we stared at each other through several resounding beats of my heart, her gaze sobered, and she straightened in her chair. My anxiety disappeared as a sense of peace gusted through me like a warm breeze on a spring day. Even though it was December and freezing cold outside.

This was absolutely right. I took a breath. "I had a plan," I began.

Her lips twitched slightly. "You always have a plan."

A smile tugged at my lips. "They're not always the best plans, though. I was going to ask you when we got home, but I suppose I'm impatient."

She blinked and pressed her glasses up on her nose. The subtle, unconscious gesture elicited a sharp, sweet twist in my heart. Because it was *so* precisely her, and it was so familiar.

I loved her so very much. I placed the box on the table between us, flipping it open with my thumb and spinning it toward her. "I thought this weekend was perfect to ask you to marry me."

I managed to speak smoothly even though my pulse had kicked up its pace again. Jane's eyes went wide, and she gasped as her palm flew to her chest. She stared at the ring before her eyes bounced back to mine. "Are you serious?"

"Of course, I'm serious." I reached for her hand resting on the table and curled mine around it. "Absolutely. I know it's what I want. So why wait? You can't even say it's too soon. We've been dating for a whole entire year, and we've known each other for as long as I can remember. I'd like for us to be together for the rest of our memories."

Just then, Sherry arrived with our drinks. Her gaze bounced back and forth between us. She let out something like a squeak before she spun away.

"What do you say?" I leaned forward. Even though I had faith in my feelings, in *us*, I'd learned that when someone matters this much, it came with a touch of awe tangled with worry.

"Yes, I say yes," Jane said firmly. She brushed a tear away when it slipped below her glasses.

"Let's see if it fits. I had to guess."

"You guessed?" she teased, her bright eyes lifting to mine.

The ring fit perfectly. "It's beautiful," she breathed.

She stared down at the ring. It was a simple white gold band with a sapphire because she told me she loved that stone. "If you don't like it—"

She shook her head quickly. "I love it."

She stood from her chair and rounded the table. I stood to meet her, folding her into my arms and holding her close.

The next thing I knew, customers were cheering, and Sherry had returned with a bottle of champagne. Dinner was much more relaxed after I got that out of the way. We returned to the house and stoked the fire so its flames were flickering through the room. We were tangled up skin to skin on the couch in front of it in a matter of minutes.

I stroked my fingers through her silky hair after we lost ourselves in each other, savoring the sense of pure sated relaxation and peace I felt only with her.

"You actually surprised me. I had no idea that was coming this weekend," she said, lifting her head and resting her chin on her curled fist on my chest.

"I'm feeling pretty good about that," I teased lightly.

She rolled her eyes. "Good. Now what are we doing for the rest of the weekend?"

"We're working on the windows." I chuckled, and Jane leaned forward, pressing her lips in the divot at the base of my throat.

"Okay. I'll do anything with you."

"Just be here with me. Well, and if you want, you can help with the windows."

She giggled. "Always."

Thank you for reading Ian & Jane's story - I hope you loved it!

Up next in the Haven's Bay Holiday Series is Joe & Thea's story.

Joe & Thea were high school sweethearts. Joe was the guy Thea was *never* supposed to fall for, but fall she did. In a tale as old as time, their parents didn't approve.

Thea left town, and Joe stayed behind. A chance encounter just before Christmas kindles the fire that never died between them.

Don't miss Joe & Thea's story - second chances for Christmas are hot, swoony & steamy!

Pre-order All We Are - due out Nov 29, 2022!

For more swoony romance...

This Crazy Love kicks off the Swoon Series - small town southern romance with enough heat to melt you! Jackson & Shay's story is epic - swoon-worthy & intensely emotional. Jackson just happens to be Shay's brother's best friend. He's also *seriously* easy on the eyes. Shay has a past, the kind of past she would most definitely like to forget. Past or not, Jackson is about

to rock her world. Don't miss their story! Free on all
retailers!

Burn For Me is a second chance romance for the ages.
Sexy firefighters? Check. Rugged men? Check.
Wrapped up together? Check. Brave the fire in this
hot, small-town romance. Amelia & Cade were high
school sweethearts & then it all fell apart. When they
cross paths again, it's epic - don't miss Cade's story!
Free on all retailers!

For more small town romance, take a visit to Last
Frontier Lodge in Diamond Creek. A sexy, alpha SEAL
meets his match with a brainy heroine in Take Me
Home. Marley is all brains & Gage is all brawn. Sparks
fly when their worlds collide. Don't miss Gage &
Marley's story!
Free on all retailers!

If sports romance lights your spark, check out The
Play. Liam is a British footballer who falls for Olivia,
his doctor. A twist of forbidden heats up this swoon-
worthy & laugh-out-loud romance. Don't miss Liam &
Olivia's story.
Free on all retailers!

Haven's Bay Holiday Series

All I Want - free on all retailers for the holiday season 2022!

All I Need - release date Nov 1, 2022

All We Have - release date Nov 15, 2022

All We Are - release date Nov 29, 2022

Light My Fire Series

Wild With You

Hold Me Now

Only Ever Us

Fall For Me

Keep Me Close

With Every Breath

All It Takes - coming Jan 2023!

Dare With Me Series

Crash Into You

Evers & Afters

Come To Me

Back To Us

Take Me There

After We Fall

Swoon Series

This Crazy Love

Wait For Me

Break My Fall

Truly Madly Mine

Still Go Crazy

If We Dare

Steal My Heart

Into The Fire Series

Burn For Me

Slow Burn

Burn So Bad

Hot Mess

Burn So Good

Sweet Fire
Play With Fire
Melt With You
Burn For You
Crash & Burn
That Snowy Night
Brit Boys Sports Romance
The Play
Big Win
Out Of Bounds
Play Me
Naughty Wish
Diamond Creek Alaska Novels
When Love Comes
Follow Love
Love Unbroken
Love Untamed
Tumble Into Love
Christmas Nights
Last Frontier Lodge Novels
Take Me Home
Love at Last
Just This Once
Falling Fast
Stay With Me
When We Fall
Hold Me Close
Crazy For You
Just Us

ACKNOWLEDGMENTS

Y'all are the best fans a girl can have! Thank you so freaking much for reading my stories, for sharing your love with other readers, for asking what's coming next, and for generally being awesome.

Much gratitude to my editor for giving this story a shine and to Terri D. for keeping me straight on the details, including the ones I forget. My assistant is super patient with me and helps make my author world go 'round.

To my early readers who sweep up anything else I missed - hugs! To the bloggers who cheer on my books and lift up the romance genre every day - thank you!

Never least, my husband and our dogs, including our new puppy who's brought a dose of joy and silliness to our home this year.

xoxo

J.H. Croix

ABOUT THE AUTHOR

USA Today Bestselling Author J. H. Croix lives in a small town in Maine with her husband and two spoiled dogs. Croix writes swoony contemporary romance with sassy women and alpha men who aren't afraid to show some emotion. Her love for quirky small-towns and the characters that inhabit them shines through in her writing. When she's not writing, you can find her cooking, counting the turtles in her backyard pond, and running with her dogs, which is when her best plotting happens. Take a walk on the wild side of romance with her bestselling novels!

Places you can find me:
jhcroixauthor.com
jhcroix@jhcroix.com

 facebook.com/jhcroix

 instagram.com/jhcroix

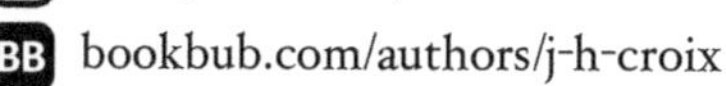 bookbub.com/authors/j-h-croix

www.ingramcontent.com/pod-product-compliance
Lightning Source LLC
Chambersburg PA
CBHW061304210726

48293CB00003B/1110